RISE OF A NEW DAWN

By Tamera Houghton Barrow

Copyright © 2013 Tamera Houghton Barrow

Printed in the United States of America

First printing, 2013

ISBN-13: 978-0615921754

ISBN-10: 0615921752

Credits: Cover - Julie Birch, Artist; Lyndsay Jones, Graphics

DEDICATION

This book is dedicated to Aunt Donna

MAY SHE REST IN PEACE.

ACKNOWLEDGEMENTS

To Julie and Lyndsay for creating the cover.

To Margaret, Indira, Jewel, and June for being my first readers.

To Blair, Cathy, and Rocky for advising me about pricing.

To Reed for convincing me that my story is different.

PROLOGUE

Dawn Hunter is the only child of Hilda and Thomas Hunter. They lived in a small community in California. Dawn's father died while she was in grade school. He was born and raised in Salem, Massachusetts. While attending college in New York, he met and married Dawn's mother. After he graduated from college, they moved to California where Dawn was born shortly thereafter.

Dawn's childhood was typical. Her parents were very protective; sometimes overly so. But, she had friends throughout her school years. After high school, all her friends went away to universities while she stayed home to attend a local college. Upon graduating from college, she worked as an accountant in a department store. Dawn always felt a "little different," but her mother would reassure her she was just "special." Thinking her mother was somewhat biased, Dawn would move along in life trying to be ordinary.

Because her father's family was back east in Massachusetts and her mother's family was in England, Dawn did not grow up knowing her families. She had such a happy childhood that she didn't realize she was missing the closeness and security of other family. She always had her pets, however; dogs, cats, a pony, and an occasional bird.

After her mother died, Dawn's life became dull and humdrum. Oh, she was personable enough and everyone at work loved her. Young people her age were few and far between. As a matter of fact, life in the small community

5

wasn't very exciting. So, she really didn't
stand a chance of any excitement. She had the
desire to create her own; just not the means.

Dawn's story begins with the mundane
routine of her life. When she receives an
invite from her aunt in England, she sees
"light at the end of the tunnel." Not only
will she finally have some closeness of family
but also maybe some excitement and adventure.
When she arrives in England, she discovers why
she is a "little different." That's when her
world changes to encompass more excitement and
adventure than she ever thought possible. So
begins the rise of a new Dawn.

CHAPTER ONE

The second-hand of the clock moves ever so close to the top where upon its arrival the alarm bells will ding their deafening chimes to indicate it is seven o'clock and time to arise. As the pendulum moves quickly between the two bells located at the top of the clock, the resulting noise arouses Dawn Hunter who is now reaching across her bed to exterminate the annoying dings. After she is awake enough to turn off the alarm, Dawn plops back down, head first, into her pillow. It is Monday morning. With a very uneventful weekend behind her, she is beginning a new week with the same dull routine.

"Why wasn't I born rich, instead of so darn beautiful?" she says jokingly to herself, "Then I wouldn't be rising so early to go to work. I wouldn't even have to work. Oh, to have some small resemblance of excitement in my life."

Jolting her back to reality, she hears the shrill chirping of her pet canary, Angus, whose sleep has also been terminated by the alarm clock. Angus will continue his perpetual chirping until he is fed, so Dawn knows there is no more sleep or even rest in her future this morning. So, she flips back the sheet and blanket to allow easier maneuvering to an upright, sitting position. She stretches both arms above her head at length until she feels invigorated enough to stand on both legs. Up she goes. Still stretching her arms as she moves, she heads towards the bird cage in the kitchen.

After feeding her pets, Dawn lumbers into the bathroom even though she is not totally awake. She prepares to take a shower where

the warm water will run through her blonde
hair and down her face. The soothing spray of
the warm water along with the blinding fog
seems to place Dawn into a state of euphoria.
For a moment, she is distant from all reality.
But, just as quickly as she looms into another
world, she returns to the reality of her dull,
humdrum life when her allotment of warm water
has turned cold. She quickly turns off the
shower water and reaches for a towel from the
hook on the back of the bathroom door. She
dries herself just enough before she slips
into a dull, blue bathrobe. She then places
the towel around her wet head to keep her hair
from dripping down her back. After she places
her feet into a pair of bright pink, piggy
slippers, she shuffles back into the kitchen.

Glancing at the clock, Dawn realizes she
will only have time to prepare some toast and
grab it on her way out. She places the hot,
buttered toast on a plate and sets it on the
table in the entry way. She continues on to
the bedroom. She rummages through her closet.
Back and forth, back and forth. As if
something different, more exciting will
magically appear with each swipe. She selects
a dress she is sure she has not worn for quite
some time. It is a navy blue dress with white
polka dots. She really doesn't like wearing
this dress. It makes her look much older than
her twenty-two years. It does, however, bring
out the blue in her eyes. She quickly
dresses, puts on her shoes, and glances at the
clock. She now realizes she only has fifteen
minutes to drive to work.

Dawn grabs her purse, the keys to her
car, and the slice of toast she left on the
entry-way table. With the toast in her mouth,
she rushes to the front door, opens it, and

turns around just as the door is about to catch her dress as it closes. She quickly grabs her dress, pulls the door closed, and locks it. She continues down the wooden stairs of the front porch leading to the driveway. With the toast still in her mouth, she fumbles through the keys to find the one to her car. She inserts the key to open the car door. She throws her purse across to the passenger side and plants herself in the driver's seat. As she reaches out to close the door, the toast drops from her mouth onto the front of her dress, butter-side down. She opens the door and brushes the toast from her dress onto the ground.

"Darn it," she complains, "My dress has a greasy spot now, and I don't have time to change. This is so typical. Just my luck. Just my life."

She continues grumbling inaudibly under her breath as she puts the key in the ignition and starts the car. Still grumbling, she backs out of the driveway. Without looking, she continues backing up into the street. The sounds of a horn and screeching brakes quickly alert Dawn that she is in potential danger of crashing into something. She applies her brakes and notices she is just a couple of feet away from a disaster. She rolls down her window and yells out an apology to the oncoming driver. She then quickly drives back into her driveway. Dawn takes a moment to compose herself. Her mind instantly reflects on memories of her mother. Since the unexpected passing of her mother five months prior, Dawn is left alone in the house she grew up in. She has wonderful memories of her mother and misses her intensely.

After the oncoming car has passed her driveway and being much more conscientious, Dawn slowly pulls out of her driveway again and into the street. Realizing that the stain on her dress is insignificant in comparison to an automobile accident, she assures herself she will get through this day and continues her journey to work.

Dawn pulls into her driveway after a busy Monday morning at work and turns off her car. She grabs her purse as she opens the car door and makes her exit. She makes her way to the mailbox where she collects her mail and walks to the front porch. She unlocks the door, slowly opens it, and walks in. She closes the door behind her and places the mail and her purse on the table in the foyer. She glances up at herself in the mirror hanging directly above the table. She looks so tired and feels so lonely. Her mind is empty and her somberness reflects her need to make her life more meaningful. Her mother had always provided not only happiness and contentment but also avenues of direction and thought-provoking guidance. But, the final decisions were always left to Dawn. Without her mother, Dawn no longer has the desire to accomplish much. She is struggling to identify a purpose in her life.

It occurs to her that she does have responsibilities. Angus is chirping a 'welcome home' song upon her return from work and is pacing back and forth on his perch. Bessie is waiting to be picked up and cuddled.

Dawn changes from her navy blue, polka-dot dress to her blue bathrobe. She slips into her pink, piggy slippers, picks up Bessie, and makes her way to the foyer to retrieve her mail. She quickly fans through the envelopes with one hand to see if there is anything worth opening. There usually isn't; only dunners. She is hanging tightly to Bessie over her shoulder with her other hand. Anticipating nothing of worth, she thumbs through them as if to just pass the time. She stops at one envelope that has caught her eye. The return address is from Ninsky in London, England. She has relatives in England but has not thought about them or heard about them since her mother died.

Dawn's mother, Hilda Fletcher, came to the United States when she was thirty years old. She met Dawn's father, Thomas Hunter, upon arriving here. They were married, and Dawn was born several years later. Hilda told Dawn very little about her family in England. She knew her mother was the oldest of three children. She had a sister, Eva, who had married a very rich man, and a brother, George. Life in the United States for the Hunter family was busy and full. There was never enough time to talk about other family members. Dawn knew very little about her father's family as well.

After placing Bessie gently on the floor, Dawn eagerly opens the letter. It is from her Aunt Eva. She writes, "Dearest Niece, You must be very surprised to be receiving this letter at this time. Since we have never met, you must be wondering how I know of your existence. I was in touch with your mother for several years before her death. She would tell me about her life and her beautiful daughter. Since I have no children of my own and my health is declining, I find myself wanting a nearness of family. I fear that you are the only family I have left. I am writing in hopes that I may know you before I am gone.

Your life is likely very happy and considerably full, but would you have time to come to England for whatever timeframe is prudent to avoid upheaval of your current stability and allow me to bestow upon you the legacy of our family. The costs for this arrangement will be of no concern for you as they will be transparent and strictly obligatory to myself. I hope this letter finds you well, and its contents will result in a mutually rewarding endeavor. Please contact my solicitor, Mr. Ed Norton, if and when you decide you are able to journey to England. He will make all necessary travel and expense arrangements for you. Contact information is provided on the enclosed card. Your loving Aunt Eva."

While reading the letter, Dawn has maneuvered herself into the kitchen. As she sits down at the kitchen table, she places the letter on the table and retrieves the three-by-five card that is still in the envelope. On it are Aunt Eva's address, phone number, and the name and phone number of her solicitor (lawyer). Aunt Eva apparently lives in Berkshire, England, but her solicitor, Mr. Ed Norton, is in London. Dawn taps the card against her fingers as her mind is filling ever so quickly with every emotion possible. Since life has been so dark and dismal since her mother died, this looks like 'light at the end of the tunnel.'

Questions are filling her brain now, "What can I expect? What will she be like? Will I be safe? Of course, she's family. Why didn't mother tell me more about her? How will I get along in another country? Is this a blessing in disguise? What have I got keeping me here? Not much. Make that, NOTHING!"

Almost as soon as she starts asking herself questions, she knows she will go. She laughs at the part in her aunt's letter where she writes, "Your life is likely very happy."

"NOT," Dawn thinks.

"And considerably full."

"Yah, full of loneliness."

Dawn tucks the card into her hands and holds it next to her heart. She begins humming and dancing around the foyer ending up in the living room. She hopes her life is about to change in a good way. She's decided it can't get much worse.

She looks up at the clock located on the bookcase in the living room. "Six o'clock," she mumbles to herself, "I wonder what time it is in London."

She shuffles in her slippers to the bookcase. She reaches for an 'Atlas' where she hopes to find a map with the division of time zones. She sits on the chair next to the bookcase with the 'Atlas' in her lap. Thumbing through the pages, she stops on the page with a large picture of the United Kingdom. At the bottom of the page is a chart that depicts time differences from specific major countries and cities. She sees that New York in the United States is one of the major cities listed. Knowing there is a three-hour time difference between California where she is and New York, she will only have to add three hours to the time listed on the chart. Since the chart indicates a five-hour time difference between New York and London, she determines there is eight hours difference in her time and London time.

"So, it is two o'clock in the morning in London," she says to herself, "It is not possible to call the solicitor now, so I will call first thing in the morning, very early in the morning."

She gets up from the chair and returns the 'Atlas' to the bookcase. She makes her way to the couch. She grabs a pillow and cuddles it to her chest. Her mind is going a million miles an hour. She begins to feel the effects of the anticipated changes to her life. The changes seem to be so drastic that she feels herself almost hyperventilating. Just as she feels herself drifting into a state of delirium, Bessie, her cat, jumps into her lap. Startled back to normalcy, Dawn returns the pillow to the corner of the couch and lifts Bessie up to her face.

"Oh, Bessie-Boo," she mushy-talks as Bessie licks her face, "Are we ready for this?"

She continues to nuzzle with Bessie until Bessie is noticeably tired of all the attention. Bessie jumps down to the floor and slowly strolls to the kitchen. With a stretch and a yawn, Dawn lays her head on the pillow on the couch, grabs a small blanket from the ottoman, and proceeds to take a nap.

The short nap turns into a total night of slumber as the ringing of the alarm clock in Dawn's bedroom penetrates her ears and interrupts her sleep. She quickly jumps up from the couch and notices the blanket as it falls to the floor. She runs to the bedroom to stop the ringing of the clock. As she pushes the button on the clock to discontinue the noise, she sits on the edge of the bed and rubs the 'sleep' from her eyes. At this moment, she realizes the importance of her habitual setting of the alarm clock. As her mind begins to adjust to normal processing, Aunt Eva's letter comes to the forefront.

Dawn looks at the clock and sees that it is a little after seven o'clock, so it must be a little after three o'clock in London. She has decided to call in sick at work in order to give herself enough time to contact Mr. Norton in London. She returns to the living room and sits in a chair next to the telephone stand. After she makes the necessary leave arrangements at work, she begins to formulate a plan for contacting Mr. Norton. First, she will make a list of all the questions she needs to ask. Then, depending upon the answers to the questions, she will schedule her time to accommodate all actions required to complete her final travel plans. Then…….

Dawn's internal mind outlining is interrupted by Bessie who is now purring her way in and round her feet. She now realizes that she needs to pursue her usual morning rituals of feeding and watering Angus and Bessie. Once Bessie's food and water have been placed on the floor for her consumption, she no longer has a need to wrap herself around Dawn's feet for attention. Knowing she can now maneuver on her own without fear of tripping over her cat, Dawn returns to the living room. She sits herself down in a chair next to the telephone table.

CHAPTER TWO

Getting herself back to the matters at hand, Dawn reflects on the outline she had previously made in her mind. Looking frantically around, she says, "Where is that card with the solicitor's phone number on it?"

She stands up and returns to the kitchen. She shuffles through the mail still on the table. She finds Aunt Eva's letter. The pages are still unfolded and opened as she left them the day before, but she can't find the card.

"Was there a card or was I just dreaming?" she thought.

She quickly picks up the letter from her aunt and begins reading the second page. Her heart flutters when she comes to the part that reads, "Contact information is provided on the enclosed card."

"Whew," she sighs with relief, "Now to find the card."

She again shuffles through all the papers and unopened mail on the table. She bends over to look underneath the table. She looks behind the salt and pepper shakers located on top of the table. She just can't find the card.

She runs to the living room. Standing right in the middle of the room, she turns slowly in a circular fashion and begins gazing at everything in the room as her brain tries to sort out where she might have put the card. Nothing comes to mind.

She moves on into the bedroom. Again, standing in the center and circling. Nothing there either. Next, into the bathroom she marches. Nada! With a sense of deep desperation, she turns and heads back to the living room.

"The last thing I remember is being in the living room just before my nap," she thinks to herself.

She sits down on the couch where she last remembers being. She looks up at the clock on the bookcase. It is now seven-thirty. If she doesn't find the solicitor's phone number soon, she will have to wait until tomorrow. She lies back against the couch and stretches herself almost straight out. She puts her hands in her pockets to keep her robe from falling to the side. To her surprise, she finds the card in one of her pockets. She pulls the card out and holds it tightly while she makes her way to the chair next to the telephone stand. She takes a deep breath and sighs with relief. She takes the receiver from the hook and begins dialing the number of the solicitor from the card. After what seems to be an eternity, Dawn can hear the ringing sound.

"Norton, Watkins and Associates," says a voice with a very British accent through the earpiece, "May I help you?"

"Um, yes," Dawn replies, "My name is Dawn Hunter, and I was given."

Before she can complete her sentence, the voice interrupts, "Oh, yes, Miss Hunter. Mr. Norton has been awaiting your call. I will put you right through. Please hold."

Dawn is speechless at the quick response from the solicitor's office. She just can't imagine anyone awaiting her call. She isn't sure now how to act or even respond.

"Well, Miss Hunter," a man's voice (also very British) is quickly heard through the earpiece, "I am Ed Norton. I am and have been for many years your Aunt Eva's solicitor. I am surmising you received your aunt's letter and are calling to make travel arrangements in acceptance of Eva's request to come to England."

"Um," Dawn begins to reply.

"Well, that is wonderful," Mr. Norton continues as if Dawn's response is rather academic, "I will make all the necessary arrangements as requested by Mrs. Ninsky. Just give me the rest of today, and I will contact you tomorrow. I am returning you to my assistant. Please give her your phone number and other information she may require. You will need a passport, and we have the means to put a rush on its delivery."

With that, Dawn can hear a click from which another voice springs from the earpiece, "Hello, Miss Hunter. I am Joyce Benson. I will be handling all the arrangements for your travel to England. You will need to go to a local, legal office with your birth certificate. Give me your phone number, and I will call you back with the information about the legal office."

Dawn gives Joyce her phone number and returns the receiver to its cradle. She sits back in the chair and gazes across the room. She just can't believe what just happened. She shakes her head as if to rearrange her thoughts, stands up, and heads towards the kitchen. She thinks some orange juice and toast or cereal will help with the gnarling noises her stomach is making.

Upon arriving in the kitchen, Dawn can see that Angus is chirping happily after satisfying his hunger with seed and water. Bessie is still chowing down with her head deep into her food bowl. She decides to have cereal today. She goes to the cupboard, opens it, and grabs a bowl and the box of cereal. She tucks the box under her arm while she tries to open a drawer to get a spoon. She puts the spoon inside the bowl and heads towards the refrigerator. She opens the door and reaches for the milk. With the cereal tucked under her arm, the bowl and spoon in one hand, and the milk in the other hand, she tries to shut the refrigerator door with the back of her body. She leans against the refrigerator to ensure that it securely closes. Slowly, she moves away to ensure her balance is stable enough to make the short trip to the table. Just as she extends her arm to lay the milk on the table, the phone rings. The unexpected noise startles Dawn just enough that she drops the milk, the bowl, and the spoon. The only thing intact is the cereal. In an attempt to run to the phone, she raises her arms slightly and drops the cereal as well. With her breakfast now on the floor, she shuffles in her piggy slippers to the living room. She reaches the phone and picks up the receiver as she simultaneously plops into the chair.

"Hello," she says.

"Hello, is this Dawn Hunter?" It is Joyce Benson, "I have some information that you will need to write down."

Dawn grabs a notepad and a pencil from the drawer of the telephone stand. She puts the pad next to the phone and reaches up to turn on the light at the other end of the table.

"Okay, I am ready," Dawn replies.

Joyce Benson continues, "You will need to take your birth certificate and driver's license to a law firm called 'Smith, Barney, and Jones.' They are located on the corner of Fifth Street and Main. They have some forms you will need to complete and sign. They will make a copy of your birth certificate and driver's license. They will take your picture for your passport. When you are done, you may return home. You must go there as quickly as possible preferably today. They will have your passport ready by the end of the week. I will be making your travel arrangements while you wait for your passport. I hope that will give you enough time to pack and get your life there in order. Someone will be in touch with you to answer any questions you have and provide further instructions and assistance." Then, she hangs up.

Dawn again returns the receiver to its cradle and sits back in the chair. She ponders in her mind all the things Joyce had said. Knowing she must work very quickly, she jumps up from the chair and heads to the kitchen. She almost steps into a puddle of milk. She looks down to see that milk is slowly oozing from the top of the milk carton. She picks up the carton and places it on the table. Luckily, the cereal box was secure enough that nothing escaped. The spoon and plastic bowl have bounced under the table away from the puddle of milk. Avoiding the puddle, she kneels down and grabs the bowl and spoon. As she arises, she also grabs the cereal box. She places everything on the table next to the milk. She goes to the counter next to the sink where paper towels are located under the cupboard. She pulls a long stream of towels and breaks them off from the roll. She returns to the puddle of milk and places the towels over the spill. The milk quickly saturates into the towels. With a circular

motion, she wipes up the milk. With each
motion, she wads the towels into a smaller
bundle to make it easier to transport to the
garbage.

After placing the wet towels into the
garbage bucket under the sink, she looks up at
the clock. It is now eight o'clock. She must
find her birth certificate, get ready for the
day, and make her way to the legal office
located on the corner of Fifth Street and
Main.

CHAPTER THREE

Her mind is going a million miles an hour.

"Where is my luggage? How much should I take? What about Angus and Bessie? What will I do with the house? My mother left the house to me. What will I do with my car? It's old and not worth much. When I get back from the legal office, I will write everything down," Dawn thinks to herself.

Returning to her senses, Dawn shuffles off to the bathroom to get ready for the day. She takes off her robe and nightgown and hangs them on the hook on the back of the bathroom door. She takes her feet from her piggy slippers and places them to the side. She removes her underwear and places them in a hamper next to the sink. She enters the shower and turns on the water. Once again, the warm water runs through her blonde hair and down her face. She drifts into a state of calm. She doesn't ever want to leave the peaceful euphoria of this moment. However, as the nice warm water turns cold, she is jolted back to reality as usual. She turns off the water and reaches for the towel. She exits the shower and begins drying herself. The mirror above the sink has fogged over, but she can still see her outline in it. She wipes the fog from the mirror with her towel. She stands there for a brief moment just staring at herself in the mirror. As water droplets begin to fall down the mirror where she wiped it with her towel, she begins to comb her wet hair. Her image is rather distorted between the droplets, but she sees a look of hope in her blue eyes that she hasn't seen before. She turns and grabs her robe from the back of the door. She puts it on one sleeve at a time as she opens the door. She moves across her bedroom to the closet where she keeps her clothes. She rummages through it as she does every day. This day, however, is different.

"What is the appropriate attire for a legal office visit?" Dawn whispers.

With the thought of just being casual, she picks some pedal-pushers and a short-sleeved blouse. She sets them on her bed while she retrieves underwear from her bureau drawer. As she puts on her underwear, she slips her feet into some flats that she usually wears with her pedal-pushers. She walks to the bed to put on the rest of her ensemble.

After she dresses, she walks back to the bathroom to dry and fluff her hair. Using the towel she left on the counter next to the sink, she wraps the towel over her hair and begins to vigorously rub back and forth. When she thinks the towel has sufficiently extracted the wetness of her hair, she removes the towel and hangs it on the shower curtain rod. She runs her fingers through her hair to separate the tangles caused by the vigorous back and forth motion of the towel. She bends over to allow her hair to flow downward towards the floor. With her hair almost touching the floor, she rifles her fingers through it to expedite the drying process by channeling air through the long strands and deep into her scalp. She then flips her head and body back upright. She arranges her hair away from her face, pulls some front strands for bangs, fluffs the sides and back; and leaves the bathroom. She grabs a thin sweater from another bureau drawer and ties it around

her shoulders. Having completed dressing, she
heads back into the kitchen.

Dawn notices the milk is still on the
table. She quickly grabs the milk and places
it into the refrigerator. She looks up at
Angus' cage where he appears to be napping
while perched on his swing. Bessie is nowhere
in sight which could only mean she, too, is
napping. Probably under the couch or under
the bed. But, no matter. Dawn doesn't plan
to be gone too long. She has much to do to
prepare for her trip.

Dawn remembers she must find her birth
certificate. She recalls using it six months
prior at work to verify her age for some life
insurance. The company gave her a packet
which she brought home and put in a metal box
in her desk drawer. She goes to the living
room where her writing desk is located in the
far corner. She opens the top drawer and
finds the metal box. She pulls the box from
the drawer and places it on top of the desk.
She opens the box and finds the packet on top.
She removes the packet. Inside the packet is
the life insurance information and, on top,
her birth certificate. She pulls out the
certificate, folds it in half, and goes to the
entry way. Her purse is sitting on the table
next to the front door. She grabs her purse
and opens it. It is still disheveled from her
almost accident the day before. She pulls the
non-essential things from her purse keeping
only her wallet, some tissues, and lipstick.
She then places the birth certificate neatly
into the purse next to her wallet. She grabs
her car keys from the bowl on the table, opens
the front door, and before departing, turns
for one more look to make sure she hasn't
forgotten anything. Confident she has

everything she needs, Dawn locks the door, enters her car, and begins her journey to 'Smith, Barney, and Jones' located on the corner of Fifth and Main.

Dawn finds a parking space right in front of the legal office building. It is a large, brown, brick building. 'Smith, Barney, and Jones' are in big white letters above the front door. After parking in her fortuitously lucky spot, Dawn exits her car and walks to the front door. She enters the building into a very large, reception area with a staircase off to the left. She walks towards the desk located in the center. As she approaches the desk, an attractive brunette looks up at her and says, "Can I help you."

"Yes," Dawn replies, "My name is Dawn Hunter, and I am here to see someone about a passport."

"Oh yes," the brunette responds, "Joyce Benson called and made all the arrangements. Have a seat, and someone will be here to assist you."

Dawn turns and walks towards a big, plush couch located next to a rock fireplace. At the same moment she begins her descent to the seat of the couch, a young man appears from seemingly nowhere.

"Miss Hunter?" the young man asks. Not waiting for a reply, he continues, "Come with me."

He begins to walk towards the staircase. Dawn follows close behind. As they both ascend the staircase, the young man turns slightly and says, "I understand your requirements are expeditious in nature. You will fill out the necessary form for a passport. I will make copies of your birth certificate and driver's license and take your picture. We will still have time to accomplish all this and get the package in the mail. The costs have all been taken care of. You should have your passport by Friday. Can I get you anything."

"A diet cola would be great, please," she replies.

No sooner does she sit down at a desk in an upstairs office than a tray with a beverage in a crystal glass and some very elegant pastries are brought in by another young man. He sets the tray down on the desk next to the form Dawn is filling out. She takes a sip of the beverage and breathes a sigh of contentment as she begins filling out the form. She completes the form and sips the last of the beverage. The first young man returns from the copy machine, picks up the completed form from the desk, and puts a collection of paperwork into a large, brown envelope.

Concluding that it usually takes much longer to get a passport, Dawn now acknowledges in her own mind the influence Aunt Eva and her solicitor, Mr. Norton, must have to ensure the issuance of her passport in such a short time. Just as the young man had outlined, Dawn completed the form, he made copies and took pictures, and the package was in the outgoing mail. The entire process takes only a half an hour. Dawn thanks the young man, descends the staircase, and exits the building. She gets into her car and begins to drive home. This whole day has been magical, so surreal. She has never been treated with such importance and elegance. She felt like royalty.

Dawn looks at her watch and sees that it is almost eleven o'clock. She is snapped back to the reality of all the things she will need to do by the end of the week. A myriad of things dances around in her mind. What was a period of smooth flowing occurrences at the legal office has now become a bunch of confusion and turmoil. How she wishes she could return to the legal office.

As Dawn makes the turn on her street and moves towards her house, she sees a black car parked in front. Staring at the car, she turns into her driveway. When she parks her car, she notices in her rearview mirror that the black car is now right behind her in the driveway. Dawn gets out of her car; and as she proceeds towards the house, she notices the back door of the car opening. A well-dressed woman who looks to be about fiftyish exits the car and walks towards Dawn. She extends her hand to Dawn and says, "Hello, are you Dawn Hunter?"

Somewhat confused, Dawn replies, "Yes, I am."

"I am Nancy Johnson," she says, "I am here to help with your departure arrangements."

"Departure arrangements?" Dawn thinks to herself, "What are departure arrangements?"

"I will help you determine what you should take to England," Ms. Johnson continues, "I will help you pack and close up the house. I will answer any questions you might have and take care of any concerns on your mind. Your Aunt Eva wants you to have no worries about your forthcoming trip. So, if we can go inside, we will get started."

Dawn blinks and slightly shakes her head. She can hardly believe what she is hearing. The feeling of such importance has now extended to her departure arrangements. She may get through this week without any worries. What a joy that would be.

Dawn and Ms. Johnson walk together towards the front porch. Dawn retrieves her keys from her purse and opens the front door. Bessie comes running into the entry way from the living room to welcome Dawn home. Dawn can hear Angus chirping from his cage in the kitchen. Instantly she wants to be assured that Bessie and Angus can make the trip to England with her.

"Will I be able to take my cat and bird with me?" Dawn inquires with a scrunch in her face at the prospect that Ms. Johnson will say 'no'.

"Of course, you can," Ms. Johnson replies with a smile.

Dawn likes Ms. Johnson for sure. She picks Bessie up and nuzzles her close to her cheek, "Hear that, Bessie? We are going on a trip."

Ms. Johnson pulls a large tablet from the case she is carrying. "Okay, Miss Hunter, she begins, "Here is what we need to accomplish. It has already been determined that your cat and bird will be traveling with you. Assuming you have no intentions of returning to work, I will take actions to provide notice to your employer of your impending resignation. I have notified a local company who takes care of house closures that you will require their services. They will come in and cover all your furnishings, turn off all utilities, board up all the windows, and make sure the house is secure. Your car will be parked in the garage in back and that, too, will be secured. Your aunt has opened an expense account in your name to be used when you arrive in England; so, if you want, you can

buy new clothes and other essentials.
Therefore, packing old personal items may be
minimized by the prospect of buying new when
you arrive in England. By all means, take
what you want to make yourself feel at home
while keeping in mind, this is a new
adventure. Do you have any questions?"

     With her mind spinning, Dawn stares
intently at Ms. Johnson. "Um, I can't think of
any right now," she replies.

     "Okay, good," Ms. Johnson responds, "I
will leave you to your packing and return
tomorrow. Here is my card if you need to get
in touch with me before my return."

     Dawn reaches for the card, places it on
the table next to the phone, and walks with
Ms. Johnson to the front door. She then
returns to the living room and plops down on
the couch. She is mentally and physically
exhausted as her world has completely turned
around.

CHAPTER FOUR

As Dawn is awakened by the ringing of her front doorbell, she sits up in bed at the realization that it is eight o'clock in the morning. Rubbing her hands over her eyes and through her hair, she wonders why her alarm did not ring. Is she so affected by the recent changes in her life that the habits she developed are now irrelevant? Forgetting to set her alarm is hardly a cause for concern that her principles are in jeopardy. She must have gone to bed exhausted and confused and simply forgot to set the alarm. The doorbell rings again. Dawn jumps from bed, grabs her blue bathrobe, and heads barefoot into the foyer.

"Coming," she yells as she finishes tying the belt to her robe.

Dawn opens the front door and finds two men standing on her porch. Behind them in the street is parked a truck with 'Hallman's House Closure Service' painted on the side.

"Hello," one of the men begins, "We are Dave and Terry Hallman with Hallman's House Closure Service. Ms. Johnson called yesterday and placed an order for us to be here this morning to help close up your house. May we come in?"

"Oh, yes, certainly," Dawn replies.

She unlocks the screen door and opens it to allow both men to enter the foyer. They quickly look around the foyer and move directly to the living room. Again, they look around before making their way to the kitchen. A quick look-around there and they continue on into the first bedroom and adjoining bathroom. Dawn follows them as they make their way down the hallway to the main bathroom and two additional bedrooms. Just as they turn to make their way back to the foyer, the front doorbell rings again. Dawn turns and heads back to the front door. She opens the door to find Ms. Johnson on her porch.

"Good morning, Miss Hunter," Ms. Johnson says with a smile, "Are you ready to get packed for your journey?"

"Please come in, Ms. Johnson," Dawn replies.

As Ms. Johnson enters the foyer, she places her briefcase on the table and opens it to extract her large, yellow writing pad. Dawn excuses herself and returns to her bedroom to get dressed. When she exits from the bedroom, she sees that Ms. Johnson is outlining for the two men the contents of the order to close the house. As Dawn overhears the instructions, she is confident that she will not have to worry about her mother's house. Ms. Johnson completes her instructions to the two men and turns to see Dawn heading to the living room. She follows and reaches the living room just as Dawn sits on the couch.

"There are some things I need to go over with you, Dawn," Ms. Johnson says as she looks at the list on her yellow pad, "Today is Wednesday. I have contacted your employer and have tendered your resignation. We are expecting your passport to be ready for pickup on Friday morning. You will have today and tomorrow to pack whatever you plan to take with you. On another note, are you aware of a book that your mother brought with her from England when she came to the United States?"

Completely taken by surprise, Dawn churns her brain for any memory of a book, "What kind of book?"

"As I understand," Ms. Johnson replies, "It is a large book with a brown, leather covering. It might look like a picture book or a scrap book."

That description didn't jog Dawn's memory at all, "I can't think of a book."

"Well, your Aunt Eva would like you to find the book and take it with you to England," Ms. Johnson responds, "It apparently has some family memories that will help you and your Aunt Eva understand your family history. I think you will know the book when you see it; so if you will look for it, it is important for you to take it with you."

"Yes, okay, I will," Dawn promises.

"I will be leaving now," Ms. Johnson continues, "So you can search for the book and start packing. The men will begin draping the furniture and securing all the windows and doors. They will dispose of all perishables."

She takes a sealed envelope from her case, lays it on the foyer table, and continues with her instructions, "Here is some spending money for you to use for food and incidentals. You can use your car until tomorrow night when they will park it in the garage and secure the doors and windows. Friday morning, I will pick up your passport and return here to retrieve you, your pets, and your luggage. There will be a private plane waiting for us at the airport. It departs at noon. You have my card. If you need help finding the book, please call me. It is important that this book return to England with you." With that, Ms. Johnson leaves.

"Book, what book?" Dawn begins to muddle the thought into her mind as she heads towards the bookcase behind the couch.

Dawns stands back far enough for a full panoramic view of all the books in the case. Back and forth, she looks on every shelf. Top to bottom and then bottom to top. Nothing jumps out at her. Ms. Johnson said she would know it when she saw it. Dawn's endeavor to locate the book is disrupted by Bessie who is now circling her ankles and meowing to assure Dawn's undivided attention. Dawn realizes that Bessie and Angus need to be fed.

After her pets are sufficiently fed and watered, Dawn decides she must start packing; so she will need to find her luggage. Dawn remembers that her mother kept her suitcases in a small storage room just off the back porch. As the men are covering furniture in the spare bedrooms, Dawn makes her way to the back porch storage room. Since she hasn't been back there for so long, she forgets that it is locked. She returns to the kitchen to get a set of keys from the key hooks next to the refrigerator. She thumbs through the keys as she walks back down the hallway to the storage room. Not knowing which key will open the door, she starts with the first key. It doesn't work; then, the next key. It doesn't work either. She continues through all the keys on the ring until she finds one that opens the door lock. As the door squeaks open, Dawn reaches for the light switch. The room illuminates to stacks of boxes and some old furniture. In the corner, Dawn can see two suitcases. They are not matching, but they are still in good condition; just a little dusty. As she retrieves the suitcases, she sees an old trunk in the opposite corner. She drops the suitcases and grabs the handle at the end of the trunk. She moves it to the middle of the room, so she can get a better look. She dusts off a metal plate just above the clasp in the front. Her mother's initials, HF, are engraved on the plate.

"I haven't seen this trunk in ten years," Dawn thinks to herself, "I thought mother had gotten rid of it. I remember she was very secretive about it. I wonder if this book Aunt Eva wants me to find is in this trunk."

With that thought, Dawn tries to twist the clasp. It won't turn. Does it need a key or is it just stuck? Dawn sits down on the floor to get an eye-level look at the clasp. There is a small hole in the middle of the clasp. It looks like a very small key, like a luggage key, might fit in the hole. Leaving the trunk in the middle of the room, Dawn grabs the two suitcases and proceeds to her bedroom. She runs to the bathroom for a towel to clean the dust and cobwebs from the suitcases before she places them on her bed. She opens them both up so she can begin placing clothes, shoes, jewelry, and personal items into the cases. Before she starts emptying closets and drawers, Dawn sits in a chair next to her bureau and begins to ponder in her mind the location of a small, luggage key that will open the trunk.

Her first thought was to look on the key hooks in the kitchen. But, trying to think like her mother, she realizes that her mother would have put the key in a special place if the contents of the trunk were of any value. Then she remembers a small box her mother kept in a drawer in her nightstand. Dawn heads down the hallway to her mother's room. The home closure men have draped coverings over the bed, the dresser, and the nightstand. Dawn removes the covering from the nightstand. She opens the drawer. She rummages through hankies, pill bottles, and a couple of paperback books until she reaches a box in the far corner of the drawer almost unreachable. She opens the box and finds a clump of hair which she knows belonged to her father, a baby tooth that most assuredly was hers, and, sure enough, a small, luggage key. She pulls the key from the box. Attached to it is a blue, satin ribbon. Dawn wraps the satin ribbon through her fingers. As she begins to close the lid on the box, her eye catches a quick glimpse of the back side of a small envelope under the hair and the tooth. With her mind submerged in thoughts of opening the trunk, she dismisses any other contents of the box and places it back into the drawer. She then heads down the hallway to the storage room.

Having left the light on, she quickly drops to the floor and seats herself, again at eye level, in front of the trunk clasp. She finds the hole and inserts the key. It fits. As her heart begins to pound, Dawn slowly turns the key. After she makes a complete turn of the key, the clasp flips clear of the lock. Dawn sits for a moment. Her heart is still pounding and her hands are shaking. She composes herself and reaches for the clasp to lift open the trunk lid. As she opens the lid slowly, she can hear the squeaking of the hinges; and the dust that falls from the lid envelops her face in a cloud of darkness. Dawn tries to swish the dust away but inhales enough to make her cough. She stands up and backs away just enough to clear the air. When the dust settles, she returns to the trunk. She looks inside to see an old table cloth her grandmother had given to her mother. She reaches for the folded fabric, but the weight of the piece requires Dawn to use both hands.

As she pulls the bundle from the trunk, the weight of something inside the cloth results in separation of an object from the fabric. With her hands full of tablecloth linen, Dawn pulls the remaining fabric from the trunk. She sets the cloth on a stack of boxes. She returns to the trunk and looks inside. To her amazement, there is a large, brown, leather book. Just as Ms. Johnson had described it except it has a leather strap around it, possibly to keep its contents from falling out.

Dawn just stands and stares at the book inside the trunk. If her heart was not pounding hard enough earlier, it certainly was now. What did Ms. Johnson say? Family memories that will help us understand our family history. Or, can it be family secrets? Oh, the thoughts that are circulating in Dawn's head. It is more than she wants to deal with right now. She grabs the book from the trunk, shuts the lid, closes the lock clasp, and returns to her bedroom. As she enters her bedroom, she notices the blue, satin ribbon holding the trunk key is wrapped around her wrist. She unwraps the ribbon from her wrist and places it on the nightstand as she passes. She places the book at the bottom of one of the suitcases on her bed and just stands there staring at the book. Thinking a break is in order, Dawn goes to the kitchen for a morning serving of caffeine. She extracts a can of diet cola from the refrigerator. She opens it as she sits down at the table. Taking several sips of her cold beverage, she reclines as far back on the chair as possible. For a moment, she is in a complete state of relaxation.

CHAPTER FIVE

Still in a state of relaxation, Dawn is aroused by footsteps in the hallway. Jarring herself back to reality, she realizes that the house closing workers are making their way to the front of the house. They have closed all rooms in the house except her bedroom, the kitchen, the living room, and the foyer. All the windows have been boarded, and the back door is locked and secured. As the workers approach the kitchen, Dawn finishes her beverage and heads to the foyer. Reaching the middle of the foyer at the same time as the workers, Dawn prepares for a progress report.

"We have completed as much closure as we can today," Dave reports, "We will return tomorrow afternoon to continue closing the house. We will be placing your car in the garage in the back tomorrow evening so you will have access to it today and tomorrow. We will return again on Friday with Ms. Johnson to totally finish the house closure."

Terry continues as Dave walks towards the front door, "Do you have any questions, Miss Hunter?"

"No, I guess not," Dawn replies, "My head is spinning from all this activity and drastic changes to my life."

Nodding his head to acknowledge understanding, Terry heads for the front door where he and Dave exit the house closing the door behind them.

Trying to decide a plan of attack, Dawn just can't seem to gather her thoughts. She assures herself it doesn't really matter right now, but she will have to work quickly and efficiently to get everything she is taking in those two, old suitcases. She heads back to the bedroom and stares again at the suitcases on the bed. She looks around the room for an alternate place for the cases. She will need the bed to sleep until Friday, so it will have to be cleared. She can place the items on top of a small dresser in a drawer and place one of the cases there. That will make it easier to empty the drawers directly into the case. She decides to place the other case on a chair next to her closet. In her attempts to rearrange the cases and get a packing strategy developed, she forgets about the brown, leather book. She clears the dresser except for a cloth runner and places the first suitcase on top. The runner will prevent scratches from the metal corners of the suitcase. She opens the suitcase again, resting the lid against the mirror of the dresser. She walks back to the bed, closes the other case, and relocates it on the chair.

Feeling as if she has been working for days, Dawn plops down on the bed for a short rest. As she looks up at the ceiling, her mind begins to reflect back on all the things that have happened since Monday. Monday – that seems like an eternity ago. She also reflects back on how dull and routine her life has been since her mother died. More excitement has happened just since Monday than has happened in many, many months. Dawn has resolved in her mind that her life will never be the same. So, if she is going to be ready for what's ahead, she will need to get started.

Dawn glances over at the alarm clock. It is now almost one o'clock. Her stomach reminds her that she did not have breakfast, and it is now after lunchtime. It will have to be a working lunch. She decides to order pizza and have it delivered. She goes to the living room and sees that the table containing the telephone has been covered as part of the house closure service. She uncovers the table to expose the telephone. She opens the table drawer to extract a small book of phone numbers that she uses regularly. She thumbs through the book and stops on the page with the number of the local pizza parlor. She calls the number and orders a medium pepperoni pizza to be delivered. After hanging up the phone receiver, Dawn replaces the book in the drawer and re-covers the entire table with the cloth. She returns to the bedroom to begin packing all the belongings she anticipates taking with her.

Starting at the dresser, she opens each drawer and transfers the contents into the open case on top of the dresser. When she has emptied all the dresser drawers, she moves to a larger bureau located against the adjacent wall. She empties each of those drawers as well. Still having room in the first suitcase, Dawn decides to wrap her shoes in plastic and place them in this case. Then, everything in her clothes closet will fit in the second suitcase. As she runs to the kitchen to get plastic bags, she is sidetracked by the ringing of the front doorbell.

"Oh, that must be the pizza," Dawn thinks to herself.

She stops in the middle of the hallway and redirects herself to the foyer. She stops at the table where Ms. Johnson has left the envelope of money. She unseals it with her index finger and opens it. To her surprise, there are bills of every denomination. There must be a thousand dollars. She retrieves twenty dollars from the envelope and places the envelope in her purse also located on the table. The doorbell rings again. Dawn quickly opens the front door. Sure enough, it's pizza. She gives the delivery boy the money, tells him to keep the change, grabs the box, and closes the door. Not only is she in a hurry, but she now realizes she is very, very hungry. Continuing her journey to the kitchen, Dawn sets the box on the table. She reaches for a napkin in a holder on the table. She opens the box and places two pieces of hot pizza on the napkin. She wipes her hands on a towel on the cabinet and opens a cupboard under the sink. She reaches down to get several plastic bags that are kept in a bucket. She tucks the plastic bags under her arm and grabs a diet cola from the refrigerator. With the empty hand, she grabs the napkin with the pizza while making her way back to the bedroom. She sets the napkin and the cola down on the nightstand next to her bed. She gets one piece of the pizza and places it into her mouth. Trying to hold the pizza in her mouth and chew at the same time, she reaches for the plastic bags. She sets the bags down on the floor in front of her closet. Finding it awkward not using her hands to eat the pizza, she sits down on the bed and eats her pizza using both hands. After eating both pieces and washing them down with cola, she returns to the closet to continue packing according to her plan.

Dawn opens the closet door and bends over to shuffle through her shoes on the floor. In the back of her closet, she finds a large, black, vinyl bag with long handles. She decides to use this bag for her jewelry and other valuables that she can carry with her.

She sets the vinyl bag on the bed and begins
wrapping her shoes in plastic bags. After she
finishes packing her shoes in the first
suitcase, she realizes that this case is now
full. She closes the lid and zips it up. She
heads back to the closet and decides to pack
her dresses first, then slacks and levis, then
blouses and sweaters. She grabs the first
dress and removes it from the hanger. She
folds the dress in half and then in half again
as she walks towards the second suitcase.
When she approaches the case, she sees the
brown, leather book. She sets the folded
dress to one side and takes the book from the
case. She places it on the bed next to the
large, black bag. She continues folding and
packing items from her closet in the order she
has decided. After placing the final blouse
in the case, Dawn looks over at the clock. It
is now after four o'clock. She closes and
zips the second suitcase. All in all, Dawn
realizes she really didn't have that much to
pack. For some reason, she thought she would
have more to show for her twenty-two years.

Feeling somewhat accomplished, Dawn's
eyes focus in on the brown, leather book she
placed earlier on her bed. Trying to recall
if she has ever seen the book before, she
wants desperately to know what's inside. She
shouldn't feel guilty about opening the book.
After all, if it is her mother's, it is now
hers. She has every right to look inside.

"How did Aunt Eva know about the book?"
Dawn is wondering. "Could the book belong to
Aunt Eva? Ms. Johnson said it had information
about family history. It is my family, too."

Dawn is having a tug-of-war in her mind.
Should she open it or should she wait until
she is with Aunt Eva? She walks towards the

bed and picks up the book for a closer look.
As she turns the book around, she notices a
small clasp attached to the strap and tucked
into the opening edge of the book. She can
barely see the three small, metal rollers with
numbers on them. It appears to be a lock of
some kind in which a variation of three
numbers will open the clasp. Well, that
certainly negates her decision to open the
book. In addition, she will now have to find
a combination of numbers that will open the
clasp unless Aunt Eva has them. It is
apparent to Dawn that the contents of the book
will remain undisturbed until she gets to
England. She places the book into the black
bag and relocates the bag on the floor next to
her nightstand. Feeling physically and
mentally exhausted, Dawn decides an early
retirement is in order. She goes to the
bathroom where she changes into a pair of
pajamas she set aside for her last two nights
in California. After looking around the
bedroom to make sure there is nothing more for
her to do, she glances at the alarm clock.
Realizing she does not need to arise at seven
o'clock, she conscientiously decides not to
set the alarm and goes to bed.

CHAPTER SIX

Sleeping very soundly for the first time in a long time, Dawn wakes up on her own. She is not jarred from a deep sleep by a noisy alarm or a door bell. She sits up in her bed and realizes how surprisingly refreshed she feels. Her mind seems to be calm and clear. Maybe she is finally accepting the changes in her life and making the necessary adjustments to embrace them. As her body recovers from the involuntary stretching, she looks over at the clock. It is eight o'clock. It has been a long time since she slept through the night and arose at eight o'clock on a Thursday. All the excitement of the previous day has certainly taken its toll. But, today she feels great.

As the incessant chirping from the kitchen gets Dawn's attention, she is aware that Angus is alerting her to the lateness of his feeding time. She makes her way to the edge of the bed, twirls her legs over the side, and places her feet on the floor. At that moment, Bessie quickly brushes her fir against her legs and meows with enthusiasm. She, too, wants Dawn's attention. It is, after all, past feeding time.

"Okay, okay, Bessie," Dawn responds as she arises from the bed, "Let's get you and Angus your breakfasts."

She goes to the bathroom to get her blue bathrobe and pink, piggy slippers. After adorning her morning wear, she shuffles into the kitchen. She first feeds and waters Angus and then Bessie. She briefly sits down at the kitchen table; and as she watches Bessie devour her breakfast, she contemplates what she will do today.

While a myriad of thoughts flows through her mind, she walks to the stove, picks up the tea pot, fills it with water, and returns it to the stove. She will, first, have some tea and toast. She makes her way to the canister which contains the tea bags. She extracts one bag and places it in a clean mug from the cabinet. She opens the bread box and realizes she ate the last two pieces of bread on Monday. So, it will have to be tea and something else. She opens the cupboard next to the refrigerator and glances up and down the shelves. She sees a box of shortbread cookies. That will have to do. Just as she arranges a few cookies on a small plate, the tea pot begins to whistle as the water inside comes to a boil. She pours the hot water into the mug containing the tea bag. Dawn relocates the mug and cookies to the table. While the tea is steeping to the perfect level of strength, Dawn returns to her bedroom to make her bed. As she covers the last pillow with the bedspread, the blue, satin ribbon on the nightstand catches her eye.

Dawn returns to the kitchen where she is confident the hot tea and cookies will be sufficient nourishment until dinner. After supplementing the tea with adequate sweetener and cream, she begins to slowly sip the hot beverage. With each sip, she becomes more alert and mindful of her options for the day. However, the more she tries to stay focused, the more her mind wonders towards thoughts of the blue, satin ribbon. She thinks of the box in her mother's nightstand. She remembers the key, of course, and the strand of hair and the tooth. But, it is now the envelope at the bottom of the box that stirs her curiosity. Leaving what's left of the tea and cookies, she arises from the table and heads towards her mother's bedroom.

Dawn enters the room and turns on the light. As she maneuvers across the room towards the nightstand, she catches her slipper on the linen covering a chair. Only a slight stumble, she kneels in front of the nightstand. She uncovers the stand and opens the drawer. She retrieves the box from the back of the drawer. She slowly opens it so as not to disturb its contents. She sets the box on top of the linen covering the stand so she can use both hands to extract the envelope. After she removes the envelope from the box, she makes sure the hair and tooth are still safely housed in the box. She turns the envelope over to read the writing on the front. It is a letter to her mother from Aunt Eva. She puts the letter in her robe pocket, makes sure all the furniture is still covered, and exits the bedroom. She turns off the light and shuts the door. She makes her way to the living room to read the contents of the letter.

As she sits in the chair next to the telephone stand, she pulls the envelope from her pocket. She opens the flap and inches the letter out of the envelope. Unfolding the letter, she can tell the letter was sent fairly recently. It is dated a month before her mother passed away.

"My dearest Hilda," it begins, "It has been almost twenty-five years since you left England. According to the legacy, you must return with the book. Only then can you undo the happenings that have tormented our family. George and I have kept your whereabouts secret in order for you to fulfill the prophecy given to you by our father. The allotted time will expire in one year, so I hope you will come home and finish what was started. Your loving sister, Eva."

"Wow," Dawn thinks to herself, "What on earth does all this mean. The legacy? The prophecy? Allotted time? Six months have already passed since Aunt Eva sent this letter. That means there is only six months left. What disaster will befall our family and what must be finished?"

If Dawn wasn't totally mind-boggled this past week, she certainly has a case for insanity now. Even in a state of total confusion, Dawn finds a certain mysterious adventure unraveling. She folds the letter and places it back into the envelope while making her way to the foyer. She must keep tight reigns on this letter. She puts the letter in a zippered compartment in her purse. She will certainly want to confront Aunt Eva when she arrives in England. Dawn tries to calm herself. Her hands are shaking and her heart is beating what seems like a hundred miles an hour. Still, the excitement of it all is giving her goose bumps.

"The book," Dawn remembers, "There must be something in the book that explains everything. Aunt Eva specifically instructed my mother to return with the book. And, Ms. Johnson was adamant that I find the book and take it to England with me. The answers are definitely in the book."

Dawn decides she will take a closer look at the book. She goes to her bedroom where she has put the book in the large, black, vinyl bag. She sits on the bed and pulls the book from the bag. She tries to think of three numbers that would open the lock attached to the strap. It would have to be a number her mother could remember. How about her birthday? May 15th – 515. Dawn tries 515. She pulls on the strap to see if it will detach. No such luck. How about Dawn's birthday? January 10th – 110. Dawn tries 110. Again, she pulls the strap. Not right either. Dawn was not born twenty-five years ago when her mother would have taken it out of England, so it is unlikely the combination would have anything to do with her.

"I could just cut the leather strap," Dawn thinks to herself.

She takes the book and runs to the kitchen. She pulls a sharp cutting knife from the butcher block on her cabinet. She lays the book on the kitchen table and tries to insert the knife under the leather strap. She runs the knife along the strap to the metal clasp. At the moment the knife blade touches the clasp, sparks of lightning-shaped fire rods bolt away from the book. Dawn can feel the knife wiggle from her hand and fly across the room landing in the sink. She instantly backs away from the table as a small, smolder of smoke dissipates. She can hardly believe what she has just experienced. Inching back to the table, she tries to find a logical explanation for what just happened. There must be magnetic components in the clasp that conflicts with the metal properties in the knife. It is apparent that no one is getting into the book without the combination.

"I hope Aunt Eva knows the magical three numbers," Dawn says out loud.

She returns to her bedroom with the book and places it back into the black bag. She is definitely not letting this bag out of her possession. She tucks the entire black bag under her pillow making sure it is concealed

completely. With all the excitement of the
letter, the book, and the fireworks, Dawn just
now realizes she is still in her robe and
slippers. She knows the house closure men
will be returning, so she promptly plans to
get ready for the day. She goes to the
bathroom to shower and get dressed.

Feeling somewhat refreshed but still
shaken, Dawn emerges from the bathroom fully
dressed but with her hair still damp. As she
towel dries her hair, she walks clumsily into
the foyer. She glances into the living room
at the clock on the bookcase. It is now
almost noon. Just as she turns back towards
her bathroom, the doorbell rings. She quickly
ties the towel around her wet head and
proceeds to the front door. She opens the
door to find the two house closure dudes on
her porch. Acknowledging their presence, she
motions them to come in. After they enter,
they immediately head towards the kitchen with
a stack of linens in hand to complete their
job requirements. Dawn follows close behind
knowing she has left dirty dishes on the table
and in the sink.

"Could you please work in the living
room," Dawn requests, "I will take care of the
dirty dishes before you close the kitchen."

With that, Terry and Dave nod their heads
in agreement and head towards the living room.
Dawn can hear them unfolding the linens and
shake them as they lay them over the
furniture. She begins to gather dirty dishes
from the table and place them in the sink.
She takes everything else from the table and
places them into the cupboards. She fills the
sink with warm water and dish detergent. She
begins to wash the dishes and silverware in
the sink and places the cleaned product into

the dish drainer. After emptying the sink of dishes, she pulls the drain stop and watches as the soap and water circles the sink and down the drain. She grabs a dish towel and begins to dry the dishes. Upon placing the last dish in the cupboard and the last spoon in the drawer, she hangs up the dish towel and heads towards her bedroom.

As Dawn passes through the foyer, she can see that the closure dudes are almost finished closing the living room. She walks to the living room to coordinate the timetable for the rest of the house. Having asked the question of their timetable, Dawn waits for a reply.

"We will close the living room, kitchen, and foyer today," Terry responds, "And return in the morning with Ms. Johnson to close your bedroom and bathroom when all your personal property and luggage have been removed. We will secure your car in the garage as the final item on the contract."

"That will be great," Dawn replies wanting to extend an air of satisfaction in their performance.

She walks back into the foyer, grabs her purse from the table, and heads to her bedroom. Having already retrieved the address book from the telephone stand in the living room, Dawn empties the contents of the drawer in her nightstand. She places everything neatly in her purse. Upon completion, she puts her purse on her bed and heads to the bathroom to remove the towel from her hair. Even though totally dry, her hair is somewhat crinkled from being in the towel for so long. After hanging the towel over the shower rod to dry, she runs a long, wide-toothed comb through her hair for a more presentable appearance. Just as she sticks her index finger in her mouth to run over her teeth, the telephone rings. Dawn knows the phone in the living room is probably covered with linen as part of the closure, so she will use the phone in the kitchen.

She quickly runs through the foyer to the kitchen. She grabs the earpiece from the phone hanging on the wall just inside the doorway.

"Hello," she says.

"Hello, Miss Hunter, this is Ms. Johnson," the voice on the other end responds, "I'm calling to see if you found the book. Alternate plans need to be made if you have not."

"Well," Dawn responds, "As a matter of fact, I did find the book."

"That's wonderful. Your aunt will be very pleased," Ms. Johnson replies.

"It appears to be a very mysterious book," Dawn replies, "It has a combination lock clasp that requires numbers to open it. I certainly don't know the combination. Anyway, I don't think I know."

Somewhat relieved that Dawn found the book but perplexed about the combination clasp, Ms. Johnson continues with departure instructions, "Regular casual wear will be appropriate attire for travel. No need to fuss with hair and makeup. It is about a nine-hour flight to England, and you will want to be comfortable. You can relax, even sleep, during the flight. We will be taking your aunt's private jet, so there won't be any holdups at the airport."

Dawn's eyes light up as she thinks to herself, "Aunt Eva's own jet. I heard Ms. Johnson say we would be taking a private plane, but I didn't realize it actually belonged to Aunt Eva."

Then, as both parties hang up, Dawn returns to her bathroom and looks in the mirror. She begins to wonder if Ms. Johnson has magical powers to see her at home. She does look a little frumpy and casually dressed. But, look what she has been through this week; not to mention the mystery of the brown, leather book. So many things to boggle her mind. No wonder her appearance has suffered with so many other things to fill her brain. But, no matter, things will hopefully mellow out tomorrow.

As Dawn returns to her bedroom, she can hear Terry and Dave finishing up in the kitchen. It shouldn't take them long to close up the foyer; then, they will again depart until tomorrow. As she shuffles around her bedroom looking for something to occupy her time, she sees the blue, satin ribbon with the key still on her other nightstand. She takes the ribbon and wraps it around her wrist. So excited about finding the brown, leather book, it didn't occur to her to see if there was anything else in the trunk. Since she has some time before dinner, she decides to take another look into the trunk. Walking past Terry and Dave in the foyer, she heads to the kitchen and grabs the keys to the storage room from the holder. She walks down the hallway as she thumbs through the keys trying to remember which key opened the storage room door. Since they all seem to look alike, she will just have to try them all again. As she approaches the door, she begins with the first key to land between her thumb and index finger. Having gone through several keys as before, she finally finds the right key. She

opens the door leaving the key in the lock and
turns on the light.

Dawn sees the trunk still in the middle
of the room. She sees the tablecloth which
surrounded the brown, leather book on a stack
of boxes next to the trunk. She forgot to put
it back in the trunk. She walks to the trunk
and kneels down low in front of it again to
get a birds-eye view of the lock. She takes
the satin ribbon from her wrist and maneuvers
the key between her fingers. She puts the key
in the lock and opens the trunk lid. She
kneels up a little to get a better view of the
contents of the trunk.

She can see the backside of a picture
frame. She picks it up and turns it over. It
is a picture of three children. The oldest
appears to be about ten years old. Dawn
thinks it might be a picture of her mother,
Aunt Eva, and Uncle George. She puts the
picture back into the trunk. In the opposite
side of the trunk in the corner, Dawn sees a
small, square, wooden box. She picks it up
from the trunk. Still kneeling over the
trunk, she decides to sit on the floor. After
making herself more comfortable, she opens the
wooden box.

Inside is a long, gold chain. Attached
to the chain is a pendant. The pendant is
also gold, but shaped rather oddly. It has a
large, yellow stone in the middle. Dawn has
never seen this necklace before. She wonders
why her mother would keep something this
beautiful tucked away in an old trunk. Dawn
puts the chain around her neck and watches as
the pendant falls just below her breasts. She
decides to take the necklace with her. She
puts the wooden box in her pocket, rises again
to her knees, and takes one more look into the

trunk. She shuffles around some cloth napkins
and some table doilies but doesn't see
anything else of significance. She picks up
the tablecloth she left on some boxes and
places it back into the trunk. She closes the
lid. Not being able to find the key on the
blue, satin ribbon, Dawn leaves the trunk
unlocked and exits the storage room.

As she walks down the hallway, she sees
Dave walking towards her. They both stop in
the middle as Dave says, "We are done for the
day. We will return tomorrow with Ms. Johnson
to finish closing the house and garage."

"Thank you," Dawn replies.

Dave steps aside and allows Dawn to pass.
They both head towards the foyer. Terry is
waiting at the door for Dave. Dawn turns to
enter the kitchen and glances back just as the
front door closes. Terry and Dave are gone,
and Dawn is feeling a little hungry. This is
her last night in the United States. She
wonders if she should splurge on something
outlandish. If she decides on something too
elegant, she will have to dress appropriately;
and all her nice clothes are packed. So, to
avoid any decision turmoil or brain clouding,
she decides to get a burger at the local 'In
and Out' drive-through. Having grabbed the
car keys and her purse, she opens the front
door and locks it behind her.

CHAPTER SEVEN

Just as she had done the day before, Dawn sleeps until eight o'clock. She barely remembers returning home from the burger drive-through and going to bed the night before. As she sits up to stretch as usual, she feels the pendant of the necklace bump against her bare belly. She looks inside her pajama top to see the gold chain hanging between her bare breasts and the pendant at the end. She pulls the chain out from her pajamas and lets it dangle on top. She grabs the pendant and cradles it in the palm of her left hand while using her right index finger to feel the texture of the yellow stone and the gold setting. She turns the pendant over and sees some barely visible indentions arranged randomly on the back of it. She tries to look closer but can make nothing out.

At that moment, Bessie jumps on the bed, meanders across, and plants herself in Dawn's lap. To make room for the cat, Dawn drops the pendant.

"How are you doing today, Bessie?" she inquires as she picks her up and kisses the top of her head.

Bessie purrs wildly rubbing her face back and forth against Dawn's cheek. Dawn sets Bessie aside, steps out of bed, and walks barefoot into the bathroom. She decides to quickly shower and get dressed before feeding Bessie and Angus. She remembers that Ms. Johnson will be picking up her passport at the law office in town this morning; and then, she will be meeting Terry and Dave at the house to ensure they complete the house closure contract. Dawn wants to be ready when everyone arrives.

As she emerges from the bathroom completely dressed, she places the necklace around her neck and tucks it inside her blouse. Believing it to have great value, she doesn't want to take any chances of losing it. She walks to the kitchen and finds the small case where one of the closure dudes put the food for Angus and Bessie. Angus' cage is on the covered kitchen table. She pours bird seed into the dish and takes the water dish and fills it with water. After making sure Angus has all he needs, she looks around for Bessie's dishes. She finds them under the table. She proceeds to fill both dishes with food and water and places them on the floor to an anxiously awaiting cat. She returns the food to the case. As she makes her way back to her bedroom, she glances at the clock in the living room. It is after nine o'clock. Striking Dawn as being the punctual type, Ms. Johnson will surely be arriving soon.

In her bedroom, Dawn collects all the items she plans to carry in the black, vinyl bag. She places all her jewelry from the jewelry box into a small, red, silk bag. She doesn't have much, so it doesn't take long. She zips the bag and places it on her bed. From the drawer of her nightstand, she takes the small, wooden box where she found the gold chain and pendant. She places it next to the silk bag. There are a couple of manila envelopes on her dresser that she retrieved from the desk in the living room before it was closed up. She places the envelopes on the bed. She gets the black, vinyl bag from the floor next to the bed and begins to place the envelopes next to the brown, leather book. She then strategically places the silk bag and the wooden box inside to ensure safe transport. She zips the large bag and sets it on the dresser next to one of the suitcases. She quickly makes her bed even though Terry and Dave will be covering it with more linen.

Just as she is about to emerge from her bedroom, the doorbell rings. She grabs the black, vinyl bag and places it next to her purse on the table in the foyer. She opens the front door. It is Terry and Dave. Dawn can see Ms. Johnson's car pulling up behind the Hallman's truck. Terry and Dave immediately head towards the bedroom where they will be making final preparations to close the bedroom and bathroom. While Dawn stands in the doorway waiting for Ms. Johnson to make her way to the porch, Terry comes from the bedroom with Dawn's suitcases in hand. He places them on the floor under the table in the foyer.

As Ms. Johnson enters the house, she hands a passport to Dawn. Dawn takes the little, blue booklet and opens it to the page with her picture.

"Well, this picture isn't very flattering," Dawn complains.

Ms. Johnson looks at Dawn with a noncommittal expression. Either she agrees with Dawn's assessment of the picture or she is just too involved in transportation plans to challenge the assessment. She looks down at Dawn's feet to see Bessie purring around in a circle.

"Do you have a crate for the cat?" Ms. Johnson asks.

"Oh, yes, it's in the coat closet," Dawn responds as she heads towards the closet.

She grabs the crate from the closet and sets it down next to the kitchen doorway. She grabs Bessie and places her in the crate. She turns to get further instructions from Ms. Johnson only to see that she has made her way out the front door to the porch. She looks out the door to find Ms. Johnson motioning to someone in the car to come to the house. The driver of the car makes his way to the porch, and both he and Ms. Johnson enter the house.

"Wait here, Nigel," Ms. Johnson directs.

Ms. Johnson grabs Dawn by the arm and walks with her into the kitchen.

"Where have your put the book?" Ms. Johnson whispers to avoid being heard by anyone else.

Not sure what trust level should be given to Ms. Johnson, Dawn decides to only divulge enough information to answer the question.

"It's in a safe place," Dawn replies, "Don't worry; it won't be out of my sight. It will not see the light of day until I am in the presence of my family."

Dawn didn't know if Ms. Johnson knew about the note that Aunt Eva had sent her mother. Judging by its contents, the note emphasized not only urgency but a certain amount of secrecy. If her mother is supposed to return to England with the book, what good is the book now since her mother is dead. There must be someone else who can use the book to finish whatever was started; maybe Aunt Eva, who is next in line.

In her mind, Dawn tries to figure out what part she plays in all this. First, she is family, and second, the only one who could possibly know where to find the brown book. Aunt Eva could not trust anyone else. So, Dawn feels a certain amount of family loyalty to share very little about the book to anyone else, including Ms. Johnson.

Not seeming to be bothered by her response about the book, Ms. Johnson exits the kitchen with Dawn close behind and directs Nigel to take Dawn's luggage to the car. Fearing he might take the black, vinyl bag, Dawn grabs the bag and her purse from the table in the foyer. With one suitcase in each hand, Nigel uses his shoulder to open the screen door. Several minutes later, he returns and enters the house. Ms. Johnson motions for him to sit down in a chair next to the front door while she heads to the bedroom to learn the status of the house closing process. As Dave throws the last linen over Dawn's bed, he informs Ms. Johnson that Terry is outside parking the car in the garage and making final preparations for securing the doors and windows. The only things left are a few items in the foyer and the front door. As Ms. Johnson returns to the foyer, Dawn is standing with her black bag and purse in the doorway of the kitchen; and Nigel is waiting to load the remaining items into the car.

Terry enters the front door and acknowledges that the car and garage are totally secured. As he waits for Dave to finish up in the bedroom, Ms. Johnson directs Nigel to load the bird cage and the cat crate into the back seat of the car. Without hesitation, Nigel arises from the chair and walks to the kitchen. He grabs the ring at the top of the cage and pulls it from the table being careful not to disturb Angus from his perch. He enters the foyer and bends down to get the cat crate. Still standing at the front door, Terry opens the screen door so Nigel can safely transport both the cat and bird to the car. Just as Terry shuts the screen door, Dave appears from the bedroom.

Placing her hand on Dawn's shoulder, Ms.
Johnson herds her to the front porch. Dave
and Terry cover the last few items in the
foyer. They lock the front door behind them
and nail a large piece of plywood over the
screen door. Still waiting on the porch, Ms.
Johnson signs the contract completion order.
She thanks Terry and Dave and bids them
farewell. She motions for Dawn to follow and
makes her way to the car. It is now ten-
thirty, and the plane is scheduled to leave at
noon.

CHAPTER EIGHT

The car arrives at the tarmac a little after eleven o'clock. Dawn is awestruck at the size of the plane.

"How many people will be on this plane?" Dawn asks.

"Only us," Ms. Johnson replies.

With that, Nigel opens the back door of the car and begins to unload Bessie and Angus. While he is transporting them to the plane, Ms. Johnson exits the car. Still holding tight to the black, vinyl bag and her purse, Dawn also exits the car. Nigel returns to retrieve Dawn's luggage, and the three of them board the plane.

The plane is very spacious. There are individual seats in the front and couches along each side in the back. Dawn can see that Nigel has placed Bessie and Angus in their own individual seats and secured a seatbelt around each one. She follows Ms. Johnson to the back and sits on one of the couches. Ms. Johnson sits on the couch on the opposite side and Nigel sits in a seat in the front. A flight attendant appears from the back of the plane.

"If everyone will fasten their seatbelts, we will prepare for take-off," the attendant says.

After securing the black bag and her purse in a storage bin at the end of her couch, Dawn looks around the couch to find a set of seatbelts protruding from the cushions. She quickly grabs the two straps and fastens them securely around her lap. She glances over to see that Ms. Johnson is doing likewise. Nigel, too, has fastened himself in. She takes a deep breath and makes herself comfortable against the back of the couch.

Dawn can feel the movement of the plane instantly. It is a very fast take-off. She hardly has time to prepare for the stomach-dropping sensation of the plane rising against gravity to ascend up into the sky. What seems like only seconds, the attendant assures everyone that they have reached their flying altitude.

"You may remove your seatbelts and move about the cabin," she instructs, "We should be landing at a private air field just outside of London at about nine o'clock this evening. I will be serving lunch, so make yourselves comfortable," she continues as she hands everyone a menu.

Dawn unhooks her seatbelt and reaches for a menu while glancing over at the storage bin to ensure the black bag and her purse are still safe and secure. She looks over the menu and decides she will have the chicken salad. While waiting for the attendant to serve lunch, Dawn looks over at Ms. Johnson who is thumbing through some papers she has extracted from her briefcase.

"How long have you worked for my aunt, Ms. Johnson?" Dawn asks.

"I have been in the employ of your family for about twenty-five years," Ms. Johnson replies, "Your grandfather hired me to help take care of the household just after your mother moved to America. With your grandmother dead, I looked after things. Your grandfather was away on business so much, he needed someone to make sure the estate was maintained."

With that, she arises from the couch and makes her way to the restroom. During her absence, the attendant appears again from the back of the plane. She demonstrates how to pull a small table from the side of the couch using the couch where Ms. Johnson was seated. Following the instructions, Dawn pulls a table from the side of her couch. Both she and Ms. Johnson are now ready to receive lunch. The attendant returns to the back and retrieves a tray full of food. The attendant places a plate with a roast beef sandwich and chips on the table for Ms. Johnson, the chicken salad on Dawn's table, and Dawn can see that Nigel has ordered fish and chips. About the time the attendant returns to get beverage orders, Ms. Johnson has returned from the restroom.

As Dawn takes the last bite of her salad and swallows the last of her diet cola, she is immediately aware of the silence. Even Angus and Bessie are uncharacteristically quiet. She wiggles her way across the couch to avoid hitting the table and arises. She walks to the front of the plane to check on Angus and Bessie. Bessie is curled up in the back corner of her crate, and Angus is asleep on his perch. Assured that all is well with her pets, Dawn makes her way to the restroom.

Dawn exits the restroom and realizes that she, too, is somewhat weary. When she returns to the couch, she sees that the flight attendant has cleared the tables and put them away. She has also provided pillows and blankets which Ms. Johnson has readily taken advantage of. Dawn takes the black bag from the bin and places it on the seat at the top of the couch and places the pillow over it. She sits down on the couch and spreads the blanket over her legs as she swings them onto the long seat. She lays her head on the pillow and almost immediately falls asleep.

Dawn starts to arouse and opens her eyes ever so slowly to see Ms. Johnson and Nigel standing over her. Nigel grabs her arms and raises her to a sitting position while Ms. Johnson grabs the black bag from under her pillow. Nigel sits on the couch next to Dawn still holding her arms. Ms. Johnson sits down on the opposite couch and begins to open the black bag. She pulls the brown, leather book from the bag as she looks directly at Dawn. Dawn can see the evil gratification in her face as she smiles. Ms. Johnson rotates the book to examine the clasp on the side. She can see it is a small, numeric lock.

"Do you know the combination to this lock, my dear," Ms. Johnson sheepishly inquires.

"No, I told you I don't," Dawn replies.

Nigel begins to tighten his squeeze around her arms.

"Give us the combination to the lock," Nigel demands.

"I don't know it," Dawn again replies.

Just as Nigel is about to become more physically demanding, Ms. Johnson intercedes.

"No matter," she says, "I will break the lock."

She reaches for a letter opener in her briefcase. She positions the book solidly on her lap and begins to insert the opener under the top strap. She slides the opener across the book until it reaches the gold clasp. The moment the opener touches the clasp blinding sparks begin to fly all around the cabin of the plane. Trying to defend himself from the flying sparks, Nigel lets go of Dawn. Ms. Johnson pushes the book to the floor and jumps, feet first, onto the couch. As the book hits the floor, the opener is jarred *loose and disappears under the couch. Dawn grabs the book and tucks it ever so tightly against her chest. Obviously traumatized by the flying sparks, Ms. Johnson and Nigel are both in a state of shock. Ms. Johnson lies down to a sleeping position on the couch, and Nigel returns to his seat in the front of the cabin. Supposing to have no further incident with the book, Dawn stretches out on her couch with the book tucked safely between her arms and chest and returns to sleep.*

"Miss Hunter, Miss Hunter," Dawn hears someone calling out her name and tapping their fingers on her shoulder.

Dawn is so surprised by the wake-up nudge, she falls from the couch clutching something in her arms. As the flight attendant grabs her arm to assist her ascent from the floor, Dawn notices she is holding a magazine. She looks frantically over at the couch to see that her black bag is still positioned under her pillow. She must have been dreaming.

"Are you alright," the flight attendant inquires bringing Dawn back to the moment.

As she nods her head to acknowledge she is alright, Dawn looks over at the other couch to see that it is empty. She turns towards the front of the cabin as Nigel looks back from his seat to see what is happening. As Dawn sits back down on the couch, Ms. Johnson appears in the doorway returning from the restroom.

"We will be landing soon," the flight attendant continues.

Dawn grabs the black bag from under the pillow and makes her way to the restroom. Once inside, she looks into the bag and gazes intently on the brown, leather book. The incident seems so real to her. She wallows it over and over in her mind. Not able to inject any evidence of reality to the occurrence, she concludes it must have been a dream. So, she refreshes herself and exits the restroom. She returns to the couch and prepares for landing. As she places the black bag next to her and fastens her seatbelt, she casually looks over at Ms. Johnson who is methodically placing papers, folders, and envelopes back into her briefcase. Ms. Johnson smiles at Dawn as she closes the lid of the briefcase and places it next to her on the couch.

Expecting the same stomach-dropping sensation of a landing, Dawn clinches her body to negate the feeling of free falling. Again, to her surprise, the landing is as smooth as the take-off. She feels the plane taxiing in another direction. She looks out the window behind her and can see a large hangar in the near distance. The plane makes a turn towards the hangar. Moments later, the plane comes to a stop.

"There will be a car waiting for us outside the plane," Ms. Johnson advises as she releases her seatbelt and grabs her briefcase.

Dawn can hear the release click of Nigel's seatbelt and glances over to see him move across the aisle to Angus' cage and Bessie's crate. With the pets in hands, Nigel heads to the front of the plane where the flight attendant has begun to open the door hatch. Dawn can see the light from the overhead beams illuminating the front of the hangar as it enters through the door of the plane. She releases her own seatbelt and grabs the black bag from her side and maneuvers her way to the edge of the couch where she gets her purse. As she rises and makes her way to the front of the plane for exiting, she sees that Ms. Johnson has already made her way to the door. By the time Dawn reaches the top of the stairway, Nigel has placed Angus and Bessie into the back of a black SUV and has opened the backseat doors on each side. Ms. Johnson hurries to the opposite side and enters the SUV. Nigel takes her briefcase and places it on the seat in the front. He then looks up towards the plane to see if Dawn needs any assistance since she seems to be lingering slowly.

"Are you coming, Miss Hunter?" Nigel inquires.

Dawn appears to be in a stupor, either from the royal treatment of landing at a private hangar or still reeling from her dream. Nigel's voice jars her out of her stupor, and she proceeds to exit the plane. As she enters the SUV, Nigel tries to take the black bag.

"That's okay, Nigel," Dawn says, "I will take care of this bag. Thanks anyway."

Dawn places her purse on the seat next to her and the black bag on the floor in front of her feet. She looks over at Ms. Johnson to make sure she has no objections to these arrangements. Ms. Johnson just smiles as she instructs Dawn to put on her seatbelt. Nigel takes his place in the driver's seat, starts the vehicle, and drives across the blacktop towards a gate opening in the large fence encircling the hangar.

CHAPTER NINE

After what seems like just minutes, the SUV pulls up in front of a hotel. Dawn looks out the window to see a large, brick sign off to the side that reads, 'Hallston Hotel.' She looks over at Ms. Johnson who is aware of Dawn's confusion.

"We will be staying here tonight," Ms. Johnson explains, "Your Aunt Eva's estate is another one hundred sixty kilometers west of here. We will stay in London for the night; and in the morning, I have arranged a trip to the beauty salon and a shopping session. Your aunt is having a garden party tomorrow afternoon to introduce you to her friends and neighbors. She expects you to arrive party-ready. Don't look so worried; you will have fun."

As Nigel opens her door, Ms. Johnson exits the SUV. Dawn gathers her purse and bag and waits while Nigel circles the vehicle and opens her door. As she exits, she looks up at the large, admirably elegant, hotel. She sees Ms. Johnson walk quickly up the front steps. Dawn situates her purse and bag, one on each shoulder, and walks quickly to the front steps to catch up with Ms. Johnson.

As they simultaneously enter the hotel through a glass, revolving door, Dawn looks around to see the ever-abounding elegance of the large entrance to the foyer. Large, crystal chandeliers enlighten the room and gold filigrees decorate the large, marble columns and fireplaces.

Even though she is awestruck at all the elegance surrounding her, Dawn finds herself following closely behind Ms. Johnson as they make their way to the front desk.

"Your suite is ready, Ms. Johnson," the clerk behind the front desk says as she slides a key across the counter. It is apparent that Ms. Johnson has been here before.

Ms. Johnson collects the key and motions for Dawn to follow as she heads towards the grand staircase. As they ascend the staircase, Dawn wonders why they don't take the elevator. Upon arrival at the top of the staircase, she understands why an elevator is not needed. Their suite is located at the top and to the left of the staircase. Ms. Johnson opens the doors to the suite as Dawn looks over the banister to the foyer below. What a view!

As she enters the suite, Dawn sees a large fireplace on the opposite side of what appears to be a living room. Two long couches are arranged on each side of the fireplace. There are doors behind each of the couches. Ms. Johnson walks left towards the door. As she opens it, she turns back to see Dawn staring intently around the living room.

"This will be your room, Miss Hunter," Ms. Johnson says.

Dawn heads over to the door that Ms. Johnson is holding open for her. She walks into the room and looks around the room as she meanders to the bed. She puts the black bag and her purse on the bed and turns around to see a slight glimpse of Ms. Johnson as she shuts the door. Dawn plops backwards on the bed and stares up at the ornately decorated ceiling. For the first time since she left her house, Dawn remembers the necklace she has tucked under her shirt. After a brief moment of relaxation, Dawn sits up and reaches under her shirt across her belly to find the pendant tucked securely below her breasts. She

glances over at the clock on the end table.
It is almost ten o'clock at night. Even
though she slept most of the time during the
flight, she finds herself a little weary. She
looks ahead into what appears to be her
bathroom. Just as she starts to make her way
to the bathroom, she hears a knock at the
door. She instantly changes direction and
heads towards the door. She opens the door to
find Nigel standing in the living room with
the bird cage in one hand and the cat crate in
the other. Behind him is a hotel porter with
her luggage in his hands.

Dawn opens the door wider to indicate her
permission for their entry. Nigel carefully
enters the room and places the bird cage on a
table in the corner and the cat crate on the
floor next to the table. The porter enters
the room and places the luggage on a small
settee located at the end of the bed. Both
Nigel and the porter leave the room as Dawn
shuts the door behind them. She realizes she
needs to find a safe place for the black bag
containing the book. She looks around the
room specifically in the vicinity of the bed.
There is a space between the night table and
the bed where she is assured the black bag
will fit nicely, and it will be just an arms-
length away while she is sleeping. She walks
to the bed and opens the black bag to reassure
herself that its contents are safe and secure.
As she reaches in to feel the leather of the
book, her fingertips bump into the wooden box
that once contained the necklace. She decides
the necklace would be safer in the box and in
the bag with the book. She removes the
necklace, places it in the box, puts the box
in the bag, and places the bag in the space

next to the bed and her purse on top of the night table.

She proceeds to the settee where she opens the suitcase that contains her nightgown. She gets the gown and heads again to the bathroom. She exits the bathroom all ready for bed. She walks barefoot across the room to the table to make sure Angus is alive and well. Sure enough, he is swinging happily on his perch. Dawn looks down at the crate and can see that Bessie is becoming somewhat restless. She opens the crate to allow Bessie an escape route. Bessie quickly runs from the crate and jumps on the bed. She prances back and forth on the bed sniffing every inch to try and find some familiar fragrance. Not finding anything familiar, she jumps from the bed and continues her sniffing ritual around the room.

While Bessie is acclimating herself to her new environment, Dawn retrieves some personal items from her suitcase. Comb, brush, hair ties, toothbrush, toothpaste, and some face cream. With her arms full of these personal items, she maneuvers her way to the bathroom and places the items on the counter. She grabs the brush to help arrange her hair away from her face. Holding all her hair in the palm of one hand behind her head, she places the wad of hair into a hair tie. She grabs a face cloth from the holder next to the sink and proceeds to wash her face. She brushes her teeth and applies a thin coat of cream on her face. She washes her hands and exits the bathroom.

She retrieves her dull, blue robe from her suitcase and tries to insert her arms into the sleeves as she makes her way to the door. She arrives at the door at the same time she

secures the opening of her robe. She opens
the door and walks slowly into the living
room. She looks around to see if Ms. Johnson
happens to be there and not in her room. As
she tries to quietly tiptoe past the mini-bar,
she is surprised by a voice on one of the bar
stools.

"Have you settled in, Miss Hunter?" Ms.
Johnson inquires.

Dawn looks over to see that Ms. Johnson
has made herself comfortable; and she, too, is
ready for bed. She is sitting with her legs
crossed on the stool making her red, silk,
pajama bottoms visible through the opening of
a white, satin robe with red, embroidered
roses. She is holding a wine glass with what
looks like a red cabernet inside. Dawn is not
a wine expert, but the vision of Ms. Johnson
casually sitting at the bar lends itself to
something as glamorous as a cabernet.

"Would you like a nightcap?" Ms. Johnson
continues not allowing Dawn to respond to her
question, "There is white wine, red wine,
champagne, and I believe there are mini-
bottles of vodka, rum, and gin, I think."

"Oh, no thanks," Dawn responds, "But a
diet cola would be good."

She heads towards the bar and starts to
maneuver behind it. She makes her way to a
small refrigerator and extracts a cold can of
diet cola. She pulls the tab on top of the
cola and begins to sip the beverage that is
spurting out from the opening as she makes her
way around to the front of the bar. She sits
on a stool next to Ms. Johnson.

Before Dawn has a chance to ask, Ms.
Johnson comments on the schedule for the next
day, "At nine o'clock, you have a fashion
showing at Herrod's. You can peruse the

fashions and select any of the ensembles you like. The party your aunt is having tomorrow is semi-formal so select something for the occasion. The attendants at Herrod's will help you determine which is formal and which is semi-formal. You will be selecting some formal wear as well because your aunt is notorious for her elegant parties and soirees. Your salon appointment is at ten, and we should plan to leave for the estate by noon. It will take about an hour and a half to travel, and I believe the party is at three or four."

With that, Ms. Johnson places her empty wine glass on the bar, slips off the stool, and heads to her bedroom. She raises her hand in Dawn's direction as if to resemble a good-night wave. Dawn finishes her diet cola, places the empty can also on the bar, and slides off the stool. Barefoot, she tiptoes again across the living room floor to her bedroom door. She opens the door and looks around the room uncharacteristically suspicious to find that nothing has been disturbed.

As she heads towards the bed, she sees that Bessie has finally found a comfortable spot on a rolled down comforter at the end of the bed. Dawn pulls the many decorative pillows from the bed and places them on a loveseat in the corner. She pulls down the sheet and blanket and sits on the edge while simultaneously swinging her legs under the covers. She slowly reclines backwards until her head is nestled into one of the fluffiest pillows she has ever encountered. No sooner does she pull the sheet and blanket up to her chin than she is sound asleep.

CHAPTER TEN

Dawn wakes up to the incessant purring of her cat against her face. She grabs Bessie and pulls her away just long enough to glance at the clock. It is a little after seven o'clock. She pulls Bessie back towards her chin and nuzzles into her neck. She is particularly rested and refreshed. She sets Bessie back on the bed and maneuvers her way out of the covers. She has not unpacked her pink, piggy slippers so she will walk around with bare feet while getting ready for the nine o'clock fashion appointment.

Dawn walks around to the front of the bed next to the settee where her luggage is half-opened. She lifts the lid of the first suitcase which contains her pants and shirts. She glances in to see what outfit might be appropriate for her trip to a top-end fashion boutique. Even her most elegant outfit is nowhere near the level of fashion she will be seeing today. But, this is all she has so this will have to do. She pulls out a black pair of slacks and a white-and-black-striped blouse. Her black pumps will look great with the slacks and Dawn feels confident she will look adequate. Dawn lays her wardrobe selections on the bed and heads towards the bathroom.

She removes her nightgown and panties and proceeds to take a shower. The shower is very large and Dawn almost feels over-exposed standing inside. She turns on the water and lets the already very warm water run from the top of her head, down her body, to her feet. She closes her eyes and just circles around as the water continually sprinkles down. Almost in a trance from the therapeutic warmth and

flow of the water, Dawn looks over at a small
shelf in the corner to find several, small
bottles. She also finds a package containing
a loofah. She has only experienced the use of
a loofah one other time. She takes the bottle
of shower gel from the shelf and squeezes a
generous amount on the loofah. She wets the
loofah and works up a rich lather before
rubbing it against her skin. Barely able to
see the loofah because of all the lather, Dawn
continues to rub it all over her body. Once
totally absorbed in the white, foamy bubbles,
she places herself under the still very warm
flow of the water. Dawn looks down to see the
lather slowly leave her body and watches it
run across the shower floor to the drain. She
washes out the loofah and places it on a hook
attached to the shelf. She reaches for the
shampoo and begins to wash her hair. The
fragrance of not only the shower gel but the
shampoo provides another level of relaxation
for Dawn outside the warmth and flow of the
shower. In her mind, she decides to stay here
forever. In reality though, she knows she
must end this perfect state of euphoria.
After rinsing the shampoo from her hair, she
finds the bottle with conditioner and amply
applies it using her fingers to reach the ends
of her long, blonde hair. She rinses out the
conditioner and exits the shower room. She
finds a towel hanging from a rack next to the
shower door. She wraps the towel around her
body and reaches for a smaller towel by the
sink to wrap around her hair. Once her hair
is securely tucked under the smaller towel,
Dawn brushes her teeth.

As Dawn leaves the bathroom, she sees
Bessie has made herself comfortable next to
the pillows on top of the bed. She walks to

the settee and opens the second suitcase to extract her underwear. She lifts up a white, lacy bra and matching panties. She lays them next to her blouse and proceeds back to the bathroom while unwrapping her hair from the towel. When in the bathroom, she briskly rubs the towel around her hair to absorb as much water as possible. She dabs the ends of her hair with the towel between her two hands. With her hair adequately water-free, she removes the towel from her body and walks naked across the bedroom to the bed. She puts on her underwear and continues to dress. Once the slacks and blouse have been installed, Dawn returns to her suitcases to find her black pumps. She remembers she placed her shoes in plastic grocery bags at the bottom of the suitcase. Reaching in the first suitcase to feel the texture of plastic, Dawn can hear the rustling as her fingers rub against the plastic bags. She pulls the first bag from under her folded clothes only to find her tennis shoes enclosed in the bag. She sets them on the floor and reaches in again. She is more successful with the extraction of the second bag. Jackpot, her black pumps are in the second bag. She takes them out of the bag and sets them on the floor.

Before she finishes dressing, Dawn goes back to the bathroom to apply her face cream and run a comb through her hair. Since she is having her hair done at a beauty parlor, there is no need to spend too much time on it now. As she runs the comb through her almost totally dry hair, she uses her fingers to fluff it and arrange her bangs across her forehead. When she feels sufficiently beautified, Dawn gathers her personal items from the bathroom and places them into one of her suitcases. Since she will be leaving after her beauty parlor experience, she needs to ensure all her belongings are securely packed and ready for transport.

After closing both suitcases, Dawn walks around the bed where she placed her black pumps on the floor. She wiggles her feet into the pumps and makes her way to the hiding place of the black bag. She reaches down and grabs the straps of the bag. She sets the bag on the bed and looks inside to make sure the brown, leather book is still securely located inside. She sees the book but reaches inside to further validate its safety by running her hand across the top. With her hand still inside the black bag, Dawn looks over at the clock to see that it is now eight-thirty. Just as she is securing the bag straps across her shoulder, Dawn hears a slight knock at the door.

"Miss Hunter," someone whispers.

"Come in," Dawn responds.

A porter enters the room followed by Nigel. Nigel has a box containing bird seed and a sack with what assuredly is a can of cat food inside. Nigel opens the box of seed and sprinkles some in the cage food dish. He opens the cage and extracts the water dish. He grabs the water dish from the cat crate and takes both of them to the lavatory. He exits the lavatory with full water dishes. He places each of them in their respective locations. When he pulls the can of cat food from the sack and opens it, the aroma arouses Bessie from her lounging position on the bed. She jumps to the floor and quickly runs to her crate where Nigel is placing the fresh can of food. Once Bessie is inside the crate to enjoy her breakfast, Nigel shuts the door and securely locks her in.

In the meantime, the porter takes Dawn's suitcases from the settee and places them near the living room door. When the porter returns to assist Dawn with her black bag and purse, she assures him she can transport them by herself. Securing the black bag ever more closely over her shoulder, Dawn walks to the table to get her purse. Black bag over one shoulder and purse over the other, Dawn walks towards the door as Nigel watches intently with every step. As she leaves the bedroom and circles the couch to enter the living room area, she notices that Nigel has left the bedroom close behind her. Ms. Johnson is in the living room area with her briefcase open on a table in the middle of the area. She is shuffling through some papers and envelopes as if to be looking for something.

"Lose something?" Dawn inquires.

"I can't seem to find my letter opener," Ms. Johnson responds.

Dawn's eyes widen as she looks directly at Ms. Johnson.

"Maybe I didn't bring it with me," she says.

With that, she closes the briefcase, latches the clasps, and, with briefcase in hand, heads towards the door. Even though it is obvious that Dawn is pondering something mysterious over in her mind, Ms. Johnson motions for her to follow. As Dawn heads towards the same door, she sees that the porter is ready to transport her luggage; and Nigel has Angus and Bessie. Ms. Johnson exits the room followed closely behind by Dawn. Looking back to see that Nigel and the porter are still part of the caravan, Dawn descends the staircase to the main foyer of the hotel. Both Ms. Johnson and Dawn exit through the glass, revolving doors to the outside where the black SUV is waiting. As she loads into the back seat next to Ms. Johnson, Dawn watches as Nigel places Angus and Bessie in the back next to her luggage. Nigel enters the driver's seat and proceeds to drive in the direction of the first stop, Herrod's.

Just moments later, the black SUV pulls up in front of Herrod's. A valet approaches the vehicle and opens Ms. Johnson's door while another valet appears from nowhere and opens Dawn's door. With the black bag and her purse securely strapped to each shoulder, Dawn walks around the vehicle to meet Ms. Johnson at the front door of Herrod's. As they both enter the department store, there are two female employees standing inside to greet them. One of the employees reaches towards Dawn and grabs the straps of both the bag and the purse. Dawn quickly jerks away.

"I will take care of these, thank you," Dawn says trying to sound appreciative.

"We can put then in the safe," Ms. Johnson assures, "They will be perfectly secure there."

The employee motions for Dawn to follow her to another room. Dawn follows and finds herself in a room with a large safe. Since the employee does not know the combination to the safe, she calls for someone else to open it. Seconds later, a large man in a black suit enters the room and proceeds to turn the combination knob. After turning the knob one way and then the other several times, the man pulls the door lever. The door opens. As the female employee and the large man stare at Dawn, she walks slowly towards the safe. She places the black bag and her purse into the safe. She backs up and waits as the man closes the safe door. When everything appears to be safe and secure, Dawn follows the female employee from the room and joins Ms. Johnson on a couch in a fashion display room. Another attendant is standing next to a curtain that drapes one side of the room from ceiling to floor.

Just as Dawn comforts herself on the couch, the drapes part and out comes four beautiful models each wearing a party dress.

"These are our most current semi-formal, party dresses," the attendant announces.

With wide eyes and opened mouth, Dawn stares intently at each model as they pass by her and circle around to the other side of the room. Once they have all passed, they stand posed in a line across the room.

"Based on the description Ms. Johnson gave us about you," the attendant continues, "Everything you see today should fit you nicely. Once you have made your selections, you may still want to try them on. Do you see anything here you like?"

"Oh, yes," Dawn replies, "I like them all."

"Very good, then" the attendant responds, "Let's try them all on."

The attendant reaches over to help Dawn arise from the couch. She leads Dawn through the drapes into a dressing room where each of the dresses just paraded in front of her are hanging on hooks. The attendant closes the door and proceeds to help Dawn remove her clothes. Standing in the middle of the room only in her underwear, Dawn watches as the attendant removes one of the dresses from its hangar. As Dawn bends over slightly, the attendant holds the dress open enough for her to wiggle her way up through the bottom. Dawn places her arms through the sleeves and turns to see herself in the mirror as the attendant zips the back closed. It fits perfectly. Dawn can hardly believe she is looking at herself in the mirror. The perfect tailoring of this dress certainly enhances the curves of her body. The bodice cinches just enough to create cleavage Dawn didn't know she even had. Her waist looks ever so tiny as the skirt of the dress flairs out in fullness. She exits the dressing room to coordinate with Ms. Johnson. For the first time, Dawn sees some emotion in her face as Ms. Johnson looks up from her briefcase and sees Dawn in the first semi-formal, party dress.

Almost choked with emotion, Ms. Johnson says, "That is lovely, Miss Hunter."

Dawn returns to the dressing room and tries on each of the dresses. With each dress, she discovers physical attributes she didn't know she possessed. Each dress is designed differently but fits her perfectly. After she dresses in her own clothes, she returns to the display room. Ms. Johnson is still seated on the couch with her open briefcase on her lap. Dawn sits beside her and makes herself comfortable. As before, models protrude from the drapery. Only this time, they are wearing very formal gowns. Instead of four models, there are a dozen. They pass in front of Dawn and again circle around to form a line. They are all so beautiful; and again, Dawn loves them all. As before, she proceeds to the dressing room and finds all the dresses on hooks. She systematically tries on each one. With each visit to the display room wearing a different gown for Ms. Johnson's approval, Dawn can see that Ms. Johnson may be changing her opinion of her. Dawn sees certain expressions on her face but can't decide if they are expressions of envy or jealousy. It was apparent that Ms. Johnson was not threatened by Dawn at all when they first met. It will be interesting to see how Ms. Johnson treats her in the future.

After she has tried on all the dresses and gowns, Dawn finds herself in the room with the safe along with the large man. He opens the safe, and Dawn reaches in to retrieve her black bag and purse. She straps each one to a shoulder and exits the room. She sees Ms. Johnson waiting at the front door. The attendant is standing next to her with a wooden clipboard. Ms. Johnson is signing a voucher.

"Send them all to the estate," Ms. Johnson instructs.

Dawn is a little surprised that Ms. Johnson does not provide more information. She does not specify whose estate, so Dawn concludes that Aunt Eva is well-known to this department store. As Dawn approaches, Ms. Johnson finishes her business with the attendant and motions for Dawn to follow. As they exit Herrod's, the SUV is conveniently waiting in front. As usual, Ms. Johnson enters the back seat while Nigel shuts the door; and Dawn circles around to the other side as Nigel follows to close her door as well. With everyone inside the vehicle, they proceed to the beauty salon.

CHAPTER ELEVEN

As Nigel maneuvers the SUV down the street, Dawn can hear Angus chirping in the back. She looks around to see Bessie peeking through the opening of her crate. She is purring and looks content. She turns back around to find Ms. Johnson looking at her. With half of a smile, she touches Dawn on her hand. Dawn is very surprised by the gesture, since Ms. Johnson has been so distant and uninterested. Not sure what she has done to deserve this newfound attention, Dawn smiles back.

Dawn's state of confusion comes to an abrupt halt as the SUV quickly stops. She looks out her window to see they have arrived at a very elegant building, castle-like. The sign on the front reads, 'Royal Day Spa and Salon.'

"Wow," Dawn thinks to herself. If she wasn't totally impressed at Herrod's, she certainly reaches the maximum 'OMG' level at this spa.

Still in shock at the elegance of the building, Dawn is unaware that Nigel is holding her door open. She exits the vehicle, and Nigel closes the door. After she is done intently admiring the building, she sees that Ms. Johnson is waiting at the front doors. With bag and purse in hand, she quickly walks to meet Ms. Johnson at the doors. Again, attendants from inside the building open the double doors to allow entrance to the two clients standing in front. As Ms. Johnson quickly walks in, Dawn follows closely behind.

Before anyone has a chance to take Dawn's bag and purse, Ms. Johnson says, "They have a safe here as well. The bag and your purse will be perfectly fine in the safe."

With that, one of the attendants grabs Dawn by the elbow and directs her down a hallway and into a small room. There is a safe in the room very similar to the one at Herrod's. Dawn is somewhat surprised at the need for so much security. Very important and probably very wealthy people must frequent these places. The attendant opens the safe, and Dawn places the bag and purse onto a shelf at the bottom of the safe. As she backs away from the safe, Dawn can see purses, boxes, and velvet bags on some of the other shelves. The attendant closes the door, twists the combination knob, and pulls the lever to indicate the safe is totally locked. Dawn leaves the room with the attendant, walks down the hallway, and joins Ms. Johnson in the foyer of the spa. Both attendants lead them through golden arches onto a wide, marble walkway. At the end of the walkway, a large, glass door opens into a huge, swimming pool area.

Entering the area, Dawn can smell the very distinct fragrance of lilacs. The attendants lead them around the pool to another glass door that opens into a room divided into individual stalls. Dawn can see that some of the stalls are occupied by women dressed in white robes and white, fluffy, flip flop-type slippers. Some of them have their heads wrapped in white towels with some green 'goop' on their face and cucumber slices over their eyes. Others are having manicures and pedicures while others are getting final touches to their makeup and hair. Dawn is again totally awestruck and can't keep her mouth closed.

Once past all the stalls, Ms. Johnson is directed into one small room, and Dawn is directed into the next room. In the room, Dawn finds a white robe hanging from a hook next to a closet. One attendant, who is still in the doorway of the room, gives Dawn directions for removing her clothes and putting on the robe and slippers. When the attendant leaves and closes the door behind her, Dawn begins to remove her clothes and hangs them in the closet. She slips off her pumps and places them on a shelf at the bottom of the closet. Still in her underwear, she places the nice, soft, fluffy robe around her shoulders and puts her arms into the sleeves. The attendant is waiting just outside the door as Dawn emerges. She can see that the other attendant is escorting Ms. Johnson to an empty stall. Following close behind, Dawn's attendant is leading her to the next empty stall.

Once seated, Dawn feels the tingling of a vibration from the chair. She is instantly relaxed and can almost fall asleep. While she waits for her treatment to begin, one attendant brings a tray of pastries and another brings a tray with juice, tea, and coffee. Once Dawn has satisfied her hunger for breakfast, an attendant begins to wrap her hair in a towel another one seats herself next to her and begins to soak her fingers in a solution. Green 'goop' and cucumbers are placed on her face and eyes.

After a facial, a manicure, and a pedicure have been completed, Dawn is ready for hair styling and makeup application. The attendant removes the towel from her hair and swings the chair around to wash it in the sink hiding under the cabinet top. When her scalp has been sufficiently massaged and her hair has been sufficiently cleaned and conditioned, Dawn is ready for cutting, styling, and makeup.

After the attendant cuts several inches from Dawn's hair, she pulls all the hair back and twists it into a roll securing it with clips. With Dawn's hair out of the way, the attendant begins applying makeup. First a moisturizer, then eye shadows and mascara, and finally a tinted foundation and cheek blush. Her hair is unclipped, and the attendant runs her fingers, using both hands, through the hair to untangle and volumize. The attendant puts a gel-like substance into her hands and applies it generously throughout Dawn's hair. After the hair is completely covered with the substance, the attendant begins to scrunch sections of the hair to create curls and waves. Using a defuser to dry the hair but keep the curls and waves intact, the attendant completes the hair treatment. Spraying the creation with a clear lacquer, the attendant swings the chair around to allow Dawn a glimpse of the final results.

Dawn looks across at the large mirror and sees an image totally unrecognizable looking back. Dawn looks around behind her to see if there is someone else sharing the mirror with her. There is no one. She glances back to the mirror and turns her head to the left to get a better look at that side and then again to the right. She can't believe this beautiful face staring back at her is her own. She sits in the chair hardly able to move. The vision has overwhelmed her. The attendant taps Dawn on the shoulder causing her to flinch.

"Is everything alright?" the attendant inquires.

Still in a bit of a daze, Dawn replies, "Oh, yes. More than all right. It's perfect. I can't believe this ugly duckling is a swan."

The attendant smiles to indicate not only a job well done but also to validate Dawn's analogy of the swan. Dawn rises from the chair, and the attendant escorts her back to the dressing room. As she passes the dressing room used by Ms. Johnson, Dawn glances in to see that it is empty. The attendant informs Dawn that Ms. Johnson completed her treatment a little earlier and is waiting in the foyer. Dawn enters her dressing room, and the attendant closes the door. She quickly dresses and then glances at herself in the full-length mirror on the wall in the room. With her beautiful face and hair, Dawn's ensemble seems to be less ordinary. She opens the door to find the attendant waiting to escort her to the foyer. As she walks behind the attendant past the individual stalls, she notices heads abruptly turn as she passes. Going through the glass door into the pool area, she is innately aware of people in and around the pool staring at her as well. But the piece de resistance was when Dawn walked through the double glass doors, through the marble walkway, and into the foyer to an awaiting Ms. Johnson. Ms. Johnson is sitting in a large, throne-like chair. Her appearance is the same as it was when they arrived; the same French-twist hairstyle and minimal makeup under her black-rimmed glasses. She turns her head slightly to see Dawn entering the foyer. She can hardly believe her eyes. She stands quickly from the chair and begins to walk towards Dawn. Dawn can see what appears to be a tear in the corner of Ms. Johnson's eye as she removes her glasses. Dawn is very surprised at this show of emotion. For a week, Ms. Johnson has been very stoic and emotionless.

"Oh, Dawn," Ms. Johnson says as she grabs her by the shoulders, "You are beautiful."

Dawn! Dawn! It has always been Miss Hunter. Dawn is taken completely by surprise. Her transformation has created a new energy in her relationship with Ms. Johnson. Still clutching to her shoulders, Ms. Johnson guides Dawn towards the room with the safe. The attendant that escorted Dawn from the spa follows them both into the room. The safe is opened, and Dawn retrieves her purse and bag. They all exit the room as two other attendants open the front doors. Ms. Johnson continues to guide Dawn to the awaiting SUV. Nigel is standing by the open door to the back seat. Glancing at Dawn and also appearing surprised by the transformation, he tries to covertly compliment the new Dawn.

"Who is this young lady?" he says with a giggle, "Is Miss Hunter staying at the spa?"

Ms. Johnson allows Dawn to enter the SUV first, and then she circles the vehicle and enters the back seat from the opposite side. She stares pleasingly at Dawn as Nigel positions himself in the driver's seat. With the vehicle started, they make their way from the spa to the main street. Once on the main route out of London, Ms. Johnson grabs a basket from the front passenger seat and places it between her and Dawn. As she opens the lid and maneuvers it to the side, it becomes a small table. Dawn looks inside the basket to see a couple of loaves of bread and a selection of meats and cheeses.

"It's after noon, Dawn," Ms. Johnson says, "You must be starving."

"It's Dawn again," she thinks to herself, "I have clearly made a friend."

"A meat and cheese sandwich will work nicely to keep hunger pains away until we reach the estate," Ms. Johnson explains, "There will be a huge array of foods at the party this afternoon, so we won't starve to death today." Ms. Johnson giggles convinced she has made a joke.

Dawn just can't believe the transformation in Ms. Johnson. Maybe there is some miracle ingredient in that green 'goop' from the spa. Even though that would be an extraordinary explanation for the personality change, Dawn is reassured that the 'new Dawn' has produced a 'new Nancy.' Dawn has called her Ms. Johnson for so long, she almost forgot her name was Nancy.

As they continue their journey to the estate, Ms. Johnson makes lunch for everyone which still seems out of character for her. She is slathering mayonnaise and Grey Poupon generously on each sandwich. As she completes assembly of the first sandwich, she nudges Nigel who reaches back to receive the rye bread delight tucked neatly into a napkin. The second sandwich is given to Dawn on a very fancy paper plate, and Ms. Johnson takes the third sandwich.

After everyone has completed their lunch, Ms. Johnson gathers everything up, tosses it into the basket closing the lid, and puts the basket back on the front passenger seat. She then sits back to comfort herself against her seat and patiently awaits their arrival at the estate.

CHAPTER TWELVE

As Nigel begins to slow the SUV indicating arrival at their destination, Dawn begins to look around through the windows to see all aspects of her new home. All she sees on the right is a tall, rock wall with black, iron prongs protruding from the top, each about two feet long and six inches apart.

"No one is going over that wall," Dawn thinks to herself.

As they accelerate a little farther, Dawn sees an end to the rock wall. A large, black, iron gate is slowly opening for their immediate entrance onto a long driveway. No sooner are they inside than the gate begins to close. Nigel waits until the gate is completely closed, and he sees a green light through his rearview mirror indicating the gate is secure; and it is safe to proceed.

As the vehicle moves slowly along the driveway, Dawn can see nothing but tall trees on each side. When the trees end, she can see a large area of green grass. They wind around the grassy area and come to a small bridge. As soon as they are over the bridge, Dawn can see a large, castle-like building in the distance.

She looks over at Ms. Johnson. "Is that Aunt Eva's house?" Dawn inquires.

"Yes, it is the main house on the estate," Ms. Johnson responds.

Even with her new image, Dawn feels somewhat out of place. It is apparent to her now that she may have to adjust her behavior to a higher level if she is going to fit in here. She refuses to tamper with her principles, so any changes will have to be transparent to everyone else. She will go along to get along for a while until she discovers her limits and her purpose for being here.

As they approach the front courtyard of the estate, Dawn sees a man and a woman walking down the front staircase. The SUV comes to a complete stop and Nigel exits to open Dawn's door. The man walks towards the door to help Dawn from the vehicle. She grabs the black bag and her purse and steps out. The man stares intently at Dawn as if he recognizes her and reaches for her arm to steady her movement on the gravel courtyard.

"Hello, miss. I am Chumley, the butler," he says as he positions her towards the woman, "And this is Ida, the maid. She will escort you into the house and direct you to your room."

As Ida grabs her by the other arm, Dawn turns to see that Ms. Johnson has exited the vehicle with her briefcase. Nigel and Chumley are retrieving the suitcases, the cage, and the crate from the back of the SUV. As Chumley heads towards the house with the suitcases in hand, Ms. Johnson walks beside him.

"Where is Ms. Ninsky?" she asks.

"She is in her room getting ready for the party," Chumley replies, "She has requested that you and Miss Hunter meet her in the library at three-thirty. Guests will be arriving at four."

Ms. Johnson increases her walking pace to catch up with Dawn. Dawn is at the top of the staircase with Ida and takes notice of Ms. Johnson on her other side as she enters the front door.

"Ida will take you to your room and help you dress for the party," Ms. Johnson instructs, "The dresses that were purchased at Herrod's should have been delivered along with some other items and placed in your room. It is now three o'clock. Your aunt wishes to see you in the library at three-thirty, so you will have just enough time to dress."

As Ida leads the way across the large foyer to another staircase, Dawn follows glancing around as she walks to catch a glimpse of anything familiar. Thinking back to the picture she found in the trunk of the three children, she was hoping to recognize the background of the picture as an indication it may have been taken in this house. There are portraits of people hanging on the wall as they ascend the staircase, but Dawn doesn't recognize any of them.

As they reach the top, Ida turns to walk down a hallway. Halfway down the hall, she opens the double doors leading to a large bedroom.

"This is your room, Miss Hunter," Ida says, "It was also your mother's.

Dawn enters the room still clutching her bag and purse over each shoulder. She looks around at the most beautiful and 'humungus' room she has ever seen. She walks over to the huge, king-sized, four-poster bed where she drops the bag and her purse. Because she must hurry to get ready for the party, a full-room walk around will have to wait. She is also very anxious to meet her Aunt Eva. She is really feeling the properness of her new environment. There was no welcoming celebration at the doorway; no pomp and circumstance as the English call it. Maybe the party will be more fun. With her recent makeover, Dawn feels more confident, more extroverted. She is surely ready for a party. Let the games begin!!

Bringing her back to the moment at hand, Ida walks towards the large doors on the adjacent wall.

"The dresses and gowns that arrived an hour ago have been placed in this closet," Ida says as she opens one of the doors, "Other incidentals have been placed in the drawers of the bureau in the corner."

Dawn looks over at the bureau. On top is a tray with gold, filigree edging and a mirror bottom. In the tray are elegant, crystal spray bottles of what looks like a different perfume in each bottle. She approaches the bureau and begins to open all the drawers. There are bras, panties, petticoats, and scarves each in a drawer of their own. Not having time to inventory all the drawers, Dawn has to decide which dress she will wear to the party; so she can collect matching underwear from the bureau. She returns to the closet where Ida is still standing. She slides each dress across the hanging bar to get a good look at the different styles and colors. She decides the yellow, flared-skirt dress with a snug bodice will undoubtedly put her in a party frame of mind. She pulls the dress from the hangar and hands it to Ida. She walks back to the bureau and retrieves matching bra and panties. Underwear in hand, she walks to the bathroom. Ida places the dress neatly at the foot of the bed and sits on a nearby settee to wait for Dawn's return.

When Dawn exits the bathroom in only the yellow bra and panties, it is obvious she is relishing in her newfound confidence. She may be in a new and strange environment, but she is going to maintain control of her own

destiny. She walks slowly towards Ida who is
still sitting on the settee. It is apparent
to Ida that Dawn is uninhibited and has an air
of sophistication about her. Something Dawn
has never had before.

Ida arises from the settee and gathers
the dress in her hands. She unzips the back
of the dress and lowers it to the floor so
Dawn can step into it. She helps Dawn thread
the sleeves up each arm and moves around the
back to zip the dress cinching it closed. Ida
follows Dawn over to a full-length mirror
standing in the corner next to the bathroom.
As Ida looks admiringly over her shoulder,
Dawn turns from side to side to get a complete
look at her entire ensemble.

"You, you are so, so lovely, Miss
Hunter," Ida stammers as she stares at the
vision in the mirror.

"Thank you, Ida," Dawn says as she twirls
and twirls across the room feeling very much
like Cinderella.

Dawn looks at the clock on the nightstand
and sees that it is quarter after three.

"Now for shoes," she says looking over at
Ida to get directions for a shoe rack.

Ida briskly walks to another closet door
and opens it. Inside are several levels of
racks containing shoes of all colors and
styles. Just like the dresses.

"I guess these are all my size, right?"
Dawn suspiciously inquires of Ida.

"Yes, ma'am," Ida replies, "They were
delivered along with your dresses and
incidentals."

Dawn sees a pair of cream-colored heels
that she thinks will look great with the
dress. Now if they are only comfortable. She
pulls them from the shoe rack, sits in a large

chair next to the closet, and places them on
her feet. Oh, they are very comfortable. She
should be able to dance all night in them,
depending upon what kind of a party this is.
There may not be dancing. Well, whatever, she
will be able to meet and greet in comfort
anyway.

She stands up from the chair and quickly
walks across the room. She glances at herself
again in the mirror. She half-twirls back and
forth to decide if her outfit is complete. It
occurs to her that the necklace with the gold-
stoned pendant would look great with this
dress. She looks over at the bed to see the
black bag still lying on top of the plush
bedspread. She walks over to the bed and
pulls the bag towards her as she scans the
room to see where Ida has planted herself.
She can't see Ida, but she can hear her in the
bathroom. She unzips the bag and reaches deep
into its corner where her fingertips touch the
wooden box. She grasps the box and pulls it
from the bag. She opens it to find the
necklace. She takes it from the box and
returns the box to its place in the bag. She
takes the bag and hides it under a couple of
very plush pillows that match the bedspread.
It should be safe until she returns. She
carries the necklace around the bed to the
bureau where there is a large mirror on the
wall above it. She places the necklace hook
between her fingers of both hands and snaps it
in place around her neck. Just as she
completes installation of the necklace, Ida
appears from the bathroom. She has Dawn's old
clothes tucked into her arms and discards them
in a wicker hamper just outside the bathroom
door. As Dawn turns to walk towards the door,
she hears a knock.

"Come in," she says.

The door opens and Ms. Johnson enters the room. She takes one look at Dawn and can barely believe her eyes. She was very impressed at Herrod's as Dawn modeled each dress and became very emotional at the spa when Dawn emerged in such beauty. Both of these put together has left Ms. Johnson speechless. This is not the young, unfashionable girl she met almost a week ago in California.

"Who are you and what have you done with Dawn?" Ms. Johnson says jokingly, "You are a vision. I just can't believe the transformation you have made. You are not only beautiful, but you carry yourself with more confidence. I misjudged you. I can see now you are a force to be reckoned with."

Dawn wonders what Ms. Johnson means by the last statement. A force to be reckoned with?? Is that a clue to her intentions? Dawn doesn't want to think about it right now. She is anxious to meet Aunt Eva. She wants desperately to know about the family legacy, the prophecy, and the other stuff she read about in Aunt Eva's letter. Dawn walks quickly past Ms. Johnson and heads towards the door. She exits and glances back to see that Ms. Johnson is following close behind. Ida exits as well and closes the door behind her. By the time Dawn has reached the staircase, Ms. Johnson has caught up to her walking step for step down the stairs. At the bottom, Ms. Johnson grabs Dawn's arm and directs her towards the library.

CHAPTER THIRTEEN

Reaching the doors to the library at the same time, Ms. Johnson opens the door and enters first. She sees that Aunt Eva is in the library. She grabs Dawn by the arm and pulls her slowly into the room. Dawn can see an image seated in a chair at the other end of the room. Knowing it is her Aunt Eva, Dawn wants to hug and embrace her. She pulls away from Ms. Johnson and begins to move quickly towards her aunt. As she gets closer, she sees that her aunt is in a wheelchair. Her aunt begins to turn the large wheels with each hand. Taken completely by surprise, Dawn slows down her gait to avoid an embarrassing collision. She stops and waits for Aunt Eva to complete her journey across the room.

"Oh, my dear Dawn," Aunt Eva says as she stops her chair just inches away from her, "You are so beautiful. You look just like your mother. Oh, how I miss her."

Aunt Eva holds both hands out in front to make way for an embrace. Dawn bends over to ensure the most tightness of a hug. For several moments, they adhere to each other. When Dawn finally pulls herself away, she sees tears have welled up in Aunt Eva's eyes. She, too, wipes away tears from the corners of her eyes. She looks intently at Aunt Eva. She starts at the top of her head with her dark hair that is arranged tightly in a bun on top. Then, she looks into the most beautiful, soft blue eyes which contrast attractively with her hair. Aunt Eva is slightly built; but because of her seated position, Dawn can't tell how tall she is. She is wearing a long, dark blue, party dress with matching shoes. As Dawn stands and backs slightly away from the

wheelchair, Aunt Eva glances at the necklace.
She motions for Ms. Johnson to leave the
library which she does quite quickly.

"I see you have on your mother's
necklace," Aunt Eva says, "I have one just
like it. Except mine has a blue stone. Our
mother gave them to us just before she died."

Abruptly changing the subject, Aunt Eva
instructs Dawn to push the wheelchair out of
the library. As they exit, Ms. Johnson has
seated herself on a long wooden bench in the
foyer. She immediately arises and takes the
wheelchair handles from Dawn and begins to
push Aunt Eva across the foyer to a wide
hallway. Dawn walks next to the chair holding
Aunt Eva's hand ever so tightly. At the end
of the hallway, Dawn can see two large, glass
French doors. As they reach the doors,
Chumley appears from nowhere and opens them.
Ms. Johnson continues wheeling the chair
through the doors and onto a large patio with
Dawn still holding tightly to Aunt Eva. At
the end of the patio, there is a rock stairway
that descends down to another patio larger
than the first. Dawn can see a large, canvas
canopy covering the entire patio. There are
tables and tables of food. Some of the guests
have arrived and are milling around, eating,
and visiting.

Ms. Johnson wheels Aunt Eva over to a
ramp next to the stairway. As she approaches
the ramp, Chumley quickly appears to complete
the navigation of the chair down the ramp onto
the larger patio. Ms. Johnson grabs Dawn's
arm to escort her down the rock stairway.
They both reach the bottom of the stairs at
the same moment Chumley arrives with Aunt Eva.
Aunt Eva reaches out for Dawn's hand as Ms.
Johnson once again takes charge of the

wheelchair. As guests become aware of Aunt Eva's presence, they begin to maneuver their way towards her. A line begins to form as each guest is welcomed by Aunt Eva and ceremoniously introduced to Dawn. When all the guests have funneled through the line, Dawn is sure she has just met over fifty friends and neighbors.

Ms. Johnson has noticeably snuck away from the reception line to evidently partake of the vast quantity and selection of food displayed on the numerous tables. Aunt Eva begins to speak in a whisper as she looks in the direction of the house. Thinking she is talking to herself, Dawn smiles and approaches her aunt to see if assistance is required. Just as she is about to approach her aunt, Ida appears and bends down on the other side of the chair to receive direction from Aunt Eva.

"Would you get me a plate of my favorites, ducky," Aunt Eva says to Ida.

"Yes, ma'am," Ida replies and turns towards Dawn, "Can I get anything for you?"

"Oh, no," Dawn responds rather jokingly, "I would love the opportunity to peruse the tables to admire and salivate over the fine assortments of food."

So, Dawn follows Ida to the table containing the dishes and silverware. She watches as Ida selects a silver tray and places a plate, silverware, a napkin, and a crystal glass on the tray. She proceeds to collect the same items for herself. As they move on to the first table full of food, Dawn's curiosity gets the best of her.

"Do you have ESP or something?" Dawn asks Ida.

Somewhat surprised, Ida responds, "No, why do you ask?"

"Well, you seem to magically appear just at the moment Aunt Eva was ready to eat," Dawn says.

Ida chuckles as she points to her ear, "We are very high-tech here. I am wearing an 'ear bug' so that Madam Ninsky can communicate with me no matter where I am."

"Oh," Dawn replies, a little embarrassed, "Then, she was whispering to you when I thought she was talking to herself."

Ida laughs at the thought of Madam Ninsky talking to herself and assures Dawn that her aunt is much too cognizant to talk to herself, as they both continue their journey around the tables. After they have piled an ample amount and variety of food onto their plates, they prepare to return to Aunt Eva. When they look in that direction, they see that Aunt Eva is no longer there. Looking around, they see that Chumley has moved Aunt Eva to a large, round table on the other side of the canopy.

Dawn nudges Ida and says, "I guess Chumley has an 'ear bug,' too?"

"Yes, we all have them," Ida responds.

As they approach the table where Aunt Eva is located, Dawn is relieved that the communication system at the estate is very modern and doesn't consist of a bunch of dinging bells. Ida places the tray in front of Aunt Eva and backs away to stand by Chumley. Dawn sits next to her aunt and smiles as she places the cloth napkin on her lap. She is aware that some of the guests are looking in their direction. Trying to ignore their stares, she begins a conversation with Aunt Eva.

"I am really looking forward to finding out about our family legacy," Dawn begins; but before she can say another word, Aunt Eva raises her index finger to her lips.

She watches as Aunt Eva pushes one of the small buttons on a bracelet she wears on her right wrist.

"There are conversations we will have that I don't want others to hear," Aunt Eva explains.

"Oh, the 'ear bugs,'" Dawn replies.

"You know about the 'ear bugs?'" Aunt Eva inquires.

"Yes," Dawn continues, "I accused Ida of having ESP until she informed me that she wears an 'ear bug,' so you can communicate with everyone. When I heard you whispering earlier, I thought you were talking to yourself."

She squinches her face to indicate embarrassment at the thought that Aunt Eva is senile enough to talk to herself. After all, she is only fifty years old. Aunt Eva laughs out loud; so loud that almost everyone on the patio can hear. Guests begin to look around to see where the laughter is coming from. Even Ida and Chumley look at each other in surprise. Ms. Johnson, who has apparently situated herself on the upper patio, peeks over the wall to see what is happening. It is apparent to Dawn that either none of these people have ever heard laughter or they just haven't heard laughter from Aunt Eva.

When Aunt Eva has stopped laughing and everyone has returned to their own business, she touches Dawn's hand and says, "You are a joy, my dear. I can tell we are going to have a wonderful time. It has been a long time since I have laughed. Your mother used to make me laugh."

Realizing this is not the time to talk about their family legacy, Aunt Eva looks over at Dawn and taps her on the hand, "We will talk more tomorrow."

At that moment, someone sneaks up behind Aunt Eva and kisses her on the cheek. Dawn looks over at the new arrival as she fills her mouth with a piece of prime rib.

"Oh, deary," Aunt Eva says, "You are late, you naughty boy; but I am so glad you came."

As the newcomer sits in the chair on the other side of Aunt Eva, he is quickly diverted to stand when Aunt Eva introduces him to Dawn. "This is my niece, Dawn Hunter," she says.

"Hello, Dawn Hunter. I am Xavier Farnsworth, but you can call me Zac. I have heard a lot about you," he says as he reaches across the table for Dawn's hand. She stands thinking he is going to shake her hand, but she is pleasantly surprised when he kisses it instead.

Dawn is speechless not only because she has just met the most beautiful man she has ever seen but also because she has a mouth full of prime rib. After Zac lets go of her hand, she sits back down in her chair. As she quickly chews the contents in her mouth, she looks over to admire the new guest. He is very tall with dark, curly hair and very brown eyes. When he smiles, a dimple is visible on one cheek.

After she has sufficiently cleared her mouth, she feels a need to respond, "Well, Zac, it is nice to meet you. Do you live around here? You seem to know my aunt well enough."

She doesn't mean to sound sarcastic, but she couldn't help noticing the very

affectionate kiss on her cheek when he
arrived.

"Why, yes," Zac says with a slanted smile
that shows off his dimple, "I am your neighbor
to the east."

"His father and mother are Lord and Lady
Farnsworth," Aunt Eva says, "Xavier has
recently returned home to care for their
estate while they are in London. He has been
in France."

Apparently, Aunt Eva doesn't call him
Zac.

"Speaking of which," Zac replies, "I must
return home. I only came over to meet the
newest addition to your family."

He reaches over and again kisses Aunt Eva
on the cheek. He stands and slightly bows to
Dawn as he prepares for his departure, "Dawn,
welcome to England. I will be back tomorrow
to see you and your aunt."

With that, he walks ever so suavely
across the patio and up the rock stairway.
When he reaches the top, he is no longer
visible. After Dawn has followed Zac's every
movement across the patio and up the stairs,
she strains her neck to just see the top of
his head as it disappears out of sight. She
glances over at a smiling Aunt Eva who is
aware of Dawn's interest in her neighbor.
Just as Aunt Eva is about to say something to
Dawn, an attractive, gray-haired man dressed
in jeans and a t-shirt walks briskly across
the patio towards Aunt Eva.

"I think I've found it," the man whispers
to Aunt Eva.

Taken by surprise, Aunt Eva motions for
the man to sit down.

"That's great, James," Aunt Eva quietly responds, "As soon as our guests are gone, we will meet you in the tech lab."

"The tech lab?" Dawn wonders to herself, "What is a tech lab?

Before James can arise to return to the tech lab, Aunt Eva introduces him to Dawn, "Dawn, this is James. He is my oldest and dearest friend. We have been together for many years." Continuing with the introduction even though James already knew about her, "James, this is Dawn."

"Hello, Miss Dawn. You look just like your mother," James says rather quickly without taking a breath.

"You knew my mother?" Dawn inquires.

"Yes. I have been a friend of the Fletcher family all my life. My father was a chauffeur for your grandfather," James replies again fast and breathless.

James arises and walks briskly back across the patio, up the stairs, and disappears much the same way Zac had done earlier.

Knowing Dawn must have a million things going through her mind, Aunt Eva discharges any further conversation by wheeling herself away from the table. As she does so, Chumley quickly walks to the back of the wheelchair to transport Aunt Eva back up the ramp and onto the upper patio where Ms. Johnson has made herself comfortable. She stands as Aunt Eva approaches.

"Nancy, will you see to the guests that are still here," Aunt Eva instructs, "Thank them for coming and make my apologies for not attending to them myself."

As Ms. Johnson makes her way down the rock stairs, Chumley pushes Aunt Eva across the upper patio into the house. Dawn is still seated at the lower patio table and sees Ms. Johnson walking towards her.

"Your aunt has other business at this time," Ms. Johnson says, "And has asked me to extend thanks to the guests. Once the guests are taken care of, Aunt Eva would like you to meet her in the tech lab. Ida will direct you."

"Well, since this affair is for my benefit, let me help," Dawn says.

Together, they approach all the remaining guests. Dawn lets them know she is glad to meet them and hope they are having a good time. She encourages them to stay and visit and eat and drink. Ms. Johnson seems to be surprised that Dawn is so comfortable already mingling with the English elite. After they have completed their social duties, both Dawn and Ms. Johnson head towards the house.

CHAPTER FOURTEEN

Once inside the house, Dawn can hardly wait to return to her room and remove her dress and shoes. Even though the shoes are very comfortable, she hasn't worn heels this high in years. Her calves have tightened slightly to the pressure of walking on the balls of her feet. She makes her way up the hallway to the foyer and over to the staircase. As she ascends the stairs, she can't help thinking about Zac. He is so friendly as well as so attractive. By the time she reaches her bedroom door, she is already anticipating his return tomorrow.

Just as she is about to open the door, she hears someone hurrying up the stairs. She turns around to see Ida as she reaches the top. Dawn waits until Ida has made her way beside her.

"Now, I don't have one of those 'ear bug' thingies," Dawn says to Ida jokingly, "So, I'm sure you must have ESP."

"Oh, no, missy," Ida explains, "Ms. Johnson told me you were on your way to your room and may need my help."

"That's okay, Ida," Dawn replies, "I can manage by myself. I promise I will hang up my dress and clean up after myself. I would like a little time for myself to take this day in. There is a lot to absorb. Could you return in about an hour to direct me to the tech lab."

"Very well," Ida says as she turns to walk away.

Dawn waves as Ida looks back to ensure her services will not really be needed.

"There is an electric buzzer on your nightstand. Buzz me when you are ready to go to the tech lab," Ida instructs.

Dawn walks in, closes the door behind her, and just leans against it as she looks around the room. The light from the outside is coming in through three, large windows on the opposite side of the room. This is the first time she has had a chance to look around since she arrived.

She walks to the closet containing her shoes, takes the cream-colored ones from her feet, and places them on the rack. She closes the closet door and systematically maneuvers her way to the next closet. She unzips the dress and drops it to the floor, so she can step out of it. She picks it up from the floor and retrieves the empty hanger from the bar. She places the dress on the hanger, zips it up, and secures the dress back into the closet. Moving on to the next closet, Dawn is hoping to find something casual to wear. Eureka! The next closet is full of slacks, levis, shirts, blouses, jackets, and blazers.

She runs her hand across the hangars containing the levis. She pulls a pair down from the bar. She takes them from the hanger and begins to put them on. They are a stretchy, denim fabric and pull up nicely onto her legs and hips. Dawn zips the front and secures the band around her waist with a rivet. She reaches back into the closet for a knit shirt. She finds a red one with a yellow sun on the front. She puts it on over her 'foofy' hair but leaves her necklace tucked underneath. Back into the shoe closet, she finds a pair of tennis shoes. She completes her ensemble with the shoes and makes her way to the nightstand to find the electric buzzer. She remembers her black bag is hidden under the plush pillows on top of her bed. She lifts the pillows and grabs the straps of the bag. She pulls it to the edge of the bed and looks around for another hiding place. She looks down to see a double mattress. She decides to hide the bag between the two mattresses. Since the weight of the top mattress makes hiding the bag there very difficult, Dawn concludes no one will bother looking for it there. She finds the buzzer and hesitates slightly before pushing down firmly.

Within minutes, there is a knock at the door. Dawn immediately walks to the door and opens it. Ida is standing there with obvious anticipation of escorting Dawn to the tech lab. Dawn quickly steps outside the room and closes the door. Ida turns and heads towards the staircase as Dawn follows closely behind. As they both reach the stairs, Dawn descends them at a quicker pace than Ida. She seems to have a renewed energy. Maybe it's the stretchy jeans or the comfortable tennis shoes. In any event, she is obviously full of something.

Dawn waits as Ida reaches the bottom. Ida moves ahead since Dawn has no idea where she is going. Ida leads Dawn down the wide hallway and turns in the middle down another hallway. At the end of the hallway is another set of stairs, much narrower than the ones in the front foyer. Up the stairs they go, Ida in front. When they reach the top, they turn and go up another flight of stairs. After ascending one more flight, there is a door with a glass window. Ida rings a buzzer that is attached to the wall outside the door. James appears in the window and opens the door. Ida moves aside so Dawn can enter. Once inside the small entrance, there is another door with a combination lock. James covers the lock with his body and begins pushing buttons. Dawn can hear the 'beeps' as James pushes one number after another. Then, a click and the door opens.

James holds the door while Dawn enters a large room with computer equipment everywhere. She stands just barely into the room while James secures the door. He walks around Dawn and moves up and around tables containing monitors and keyboards. Dawn slowly follows trying not to stumble on the massive array of cords and cables. On the other side of the tables, there is one large monitor on the wall with one keyboard on a desk and a chair in front. James sits in the chair and begins maneuvering the mouse to display a web-like graph on the monitor. On the opposite side of the room is an elevator door. Dawn is a little surprised, even though she shouldn't be, to see an elevator door; but she realizes it must be Aunt Eva's means for transport to the tech lab.

Staring up at the monitor trying to decipher its contents, Dawn suddenly hears a motor running. Looking around to see the source of the noise, she is startled by the abrupt opening of the elevator door. Aunt Eva emerges from the elevator wheeling herself down a small ramp into the area where James is sitting in front of the monitor.

"Well, James," Aunt Eva says as she wheels closer to the desk, "Let's see what you have found."

James pushes a button to lighten up the graph, "See that small, blinking light in the lower left-hand corner of the graph."

Aunt Eva stretches her neck in the direction of the monitor and squints her eyes to make the view less blurry. Dawn moves closer to the desk to also get a better look. Both Aunt Eva and Dawn acknowledge they can see the faint blinking of a light.

"Well," James says, "I believe that is George's 'ear bug.' So it is still active. However, it has not moved for several hours."

"George?" Dawn glances at Aunt Eva with a puzzled look.

"Yes, your Uncle George," Aunt Eva explains, "He is my younger brother, and of course, your mother's brother. For you to totally understand any of this, we need to start at the beginning."

Aunt Eva turns her chair away from the desk while James gets another chair and places it behind Dawn. Dawn sits down in the chair and gazes intently at Aunt Eva. James sits in the swivel chair in front of the monitor and turns the chair around to form the third part of a triangle with Dawn and Aunt Eva. Aunt Eva sits back firmly against her wheelchair and begins her story.

"Back in the eighteen century, the 1700s, the Fletcher family owned all the property on the south side of the river west of London which today is all of Berkshire. Our ancestors worked the land and provided support to the inhabitants of London by monitoring the road going through Berkshire for travelers, specifically enemies of the crown, coming from the west. They also monitored the waterways for travelers on the river.

Even though our family had been accused of using witchcraft on many occasions, nothing was ever proven. Because of the protection the Fletcher clan provided to London from enemies in the west, many happenings were overlooked. Anyway, to get to the point, we are a family of witches and wizards. Magical spells and potions have been passed down from generation to generation. The oldest of each generation was given the majority of the power, but combined with other siblings, the power was even stronger. My father was the oldest of his generation and had very powerful magic but didn't use it significantly in these modern days. My mother, however, also the oldest came from Surrey where magic was practiced more frequently. So, between my father and mother, there was an abundance of magical energy in our household. My father tried to subdue it, but my mother wished to use it."

Dawn's eyes are as big as saucers, and they hardly blink throughout the whole story. She is obviously in a state of disbelief; however, Aunt Eva continues.

"My father would get rid of any written signs of magic to include all books, diaries, and journals left to him by his family. But, my mother brought a brown, leather book with her from Surrey when she married my father. It contained writings from previous generations of witches and wizards. She and my father added writings to it throughout the years until father realized the dangers of using magic. My mother hid the book when my father began burning magical documentation. That is the book you have brought with you, Dawn. Your mother took the book with her to the United States when she left almost twenty-five years ago and hopefully added her own writings to it. The book contains some very powerful magic; and if anyone outside the family knows of its existence, we could be in significant danger."

Dawn arises from her chair and circles around it rubbing her hands together intensely. Knowing there is more to this story, she promptly sits back down. Aunt Eva takes the queue and continues with the story.

"Since your mother was the oldest, she excelled in practicing magic. My mother doted on Hilda and spent many hours, out of the purview of my father, teaching magic to her. She spent some time teaching me, but I didn't have near the magical capabilities that Hilda had. For fear of getting caught by my father, neither my mother nor Hilda dared practice magic in any great length. Maybe when he was out of town, they would adjourn to the basement and whip up a spell or two. I and George would occasionally go with them."

Aunt Eva laughs out loud as she recalls, "Once your mother turned George into a rabbit."

Dawn laughs and is now very intrigued by this outlandish story. She looks at Aunt Eva as if to say, "Tell me more."

"Well," Aunt Eva goes on, "Over the years, your mother became very proficient at magic. However, she was very uncomfortable using it not only because our father forbade the use of it but also because it could do so much damage if used inappropriately. So, magic was nonexistent here for a long time. As fate would have it though, a witch named Elsa from Surrey came up to visit my mother. She apparently had some vendetta against my mother. The witch showed up one day while my mother, Hilda, and I were out in the back garden next to the large hedge that extends from one end of the property line, against the river, to the other end of the property line. I had just gotten married the year before and was home visiting while my husband was away on business. As the witch approached, I could

see the fire in her eyes. Her hands and arms
were circling and jerking profusely while she
was chanting something unrecognizable. Her
arms suddenly stopped moving and became still
in an outstretched position. A visible wave
of energy flowed from her fingertips in the
direction of my mother. I tried to move
quickly towards my mother to position myself
between her and the obvious incoming danger.
I tripped on a small rose bush and hit my head
on the ground. The wave of energy went over
me and directly into my mother. She was
thrown back over a lilac tree and onto the
lawn. Hilda, whose back was towards the witch
when she approached us, quickly turned around
and instinctively threw her arms outwards,
saying something in rhyme as sparks emitted
from her fingers into the witch. The witch
was frozen from motion but began to make loud
and fearful threats. Using another spell,
Hilda motioned her hands in the direction of
the hedge; and the witch was thrown into it.
Before the witch could escape the hedge, Hilda
again recited another rhyme and raised her
arms as if to consume the entire hedge.
Viola! The hedge had become a prison for the
maniacal witch."

Convinced this is just a bedtime story,
Dawn situates herself a little more
comfortably in her chair. Without going into
any more detail today, Aunt Eva elaborates on
the bottom line.

"Our mother died in the attack, I have
been in this wheelchair ever since, and there
is a witch imprisoned in our hedge in the back
of this estate. Hilda was so overcome by the
magical energy required to subdue the witch
and toss her into the hedge that she could
barely move for several hours. Our mother was

dead, I was destined to live in a wheelchair, and the witch would attack our entire family if she got out of the hedge. Even though our father swore he wouldn't use magic, he was so distraught over the death of his wife; he conjured up a spell that would keep the witch imprisoned in the hedge for twenty-five years. After that, the witch would have to be killed. Knowing that your mother had the genetic powers to cast a fatal spell on the witch, our father sent your mother to the United States to keep her safe. She was destined to return just before the twenty-five years were up to fulfill the prophecy outlined by our father. So, Dawn, that is why you are here."

"Me?" Dawn says with a very confused look on her face, "What can I do? Even if I believe this story, how can I do magic?"

"You are the first born of a first born," Aunt Eva explains, "Your grandfather and grandmother were highly endowed with magic in their own right. Together, they could have been undefeatable. Your mother had the genes of both. Magic is inherited whether it is actively used or not. It just takes a little knowledge and practice. You have the brown, leather book, and that's all you need. Also, your mother predicted you would be the one to fulfill the family legacy."

Dawn stands up from the chair and again circles it scratching the top of her head. Nothing else that has happened to her in the last week will even compare to the story she has just been told. As Aunt Eva begins to wheel her chair around in the direction of the ramp leading to the elevator, she turns for one last instruction.

"We will only speak of this in this room. It is sound-proof and securely locked," she says, "Retire for the evening, and we will talk more tomorrow after breakfast. No one, but you and I and James, knows the value of the book. Please keep it safe until we are able to know its contents."

Aunt Eva wheels herself up the ramp and backs into the elevator. The door closes, the motor runs, and Aunt Eva is lowered to the main floor. James escorts Dawn to the other exit doors. As he opens the second door, Dawn can see Ida standing outside. She exits the tech lab and follows Ida down the stairs. She walks quietly behind as Ida leads the way to the bedroom.

"Do you need any help, Miss Hunter?" Ida says as she opens the bedroom door.

"No, thanks, Ida," Dawn replies feeling very melancholy, "I can manage myself. Good night."

She walks past Ida and closes the door.

CHAPTER FIFTEEN

Dawn awakes on her own. No knocks, no bells, no buzzers. She sits up on the massive bed and looks over at the clock on the nightstand. It is after eight o'clock. It seems to be quite late in the morning to be arising, but Dawn can't seem to remember what time she fell asleep. As a matter of fact, she can't remember changing her clothes or getting into bed. The last she remembers is saying 'Good Night' to Ida. She climbs out of bed and walks barefoot into the bathroom. The floor is a little chilly, so she makes a mental note to remember to get her piggy slippers from her suitcase. Seeing a yellow satin robe hanging from the hook on the back of the bathroom door, Dawn decides to take a shower now instead of waiting until she has unpacked her suitcases to get her own robe. Looking around the room, she realizes she will have the same great showering experience she had at the Hallston Hotel in London.

Dawn exits the bathroom wearing the yellow robe and fluffy white towel around her wet hair. She goes to the bureau to retrieve some new underwear. Knowing that Zac will be visiting today, she wants to look her best. That means 'foofy' hair and great makeup. She is not real experienced in doing either but thinks she watched close enough to do an adequate job herself. Her feet are still cold on the floor, but she can't seem to locate her suitcases. She goes to the shoe closet to see if there are slippers in there. Sure enough, lovely, white slippers on the bottom rack. She takes them out and places them on her feet. Much better!

She walks across the floor in the new
slippers to the closet with the casual wear.
She thinks some nice slacks and a sweater will
be appropriate attire for the day. However,
now knowing what Aunt Eva has in store for
her, she may never be able to determine
'appropriate attire.' Nonetheless, she pulls
some black slacks and a blue, tight-knit,
turtleneck sweater from the closet. She lays
them neatly at the foot of the bed. She
decides she will dress before doing her hair
and makeup so the turtleneck sweater doesn't
damage her attempt to be glamorous. She takes
the towel from her head and ruffles it over
her hair to achieve as much drying as
possible. She fingers her hair back and away
from her face. She gets dressed and walks to
the shoe closet to switch her white slippers
for some shoes to wear with slacks. She finds
a great pair of flat, black, leather ankle-
boots that zip up the side.

"These will be perfect," Dawn says to
herself, "Someone around here has great taste.
Couldn't be Ms. Johnson. Maybe someone at
Herrod's. Anyway, I'm lookin' good and
feelin' great."

After putting on the boots and admiring
them in the full-length mirror, Dawn retreats
to the bathroom hoping there are products to
do her hair and makeup. In the far corner of
the bathroom, there is a long, makeup table
with a mirror right in the middle. There is a
chair on wheels in front and drawers on each
side. Dawn sits down in the chair and turns
on the lights that encircle the mirror. She
opens the top drawer on the right to find a
layered tray with eye pencils, eye shadows,
and mascara. In the next drawer is a tray
with foundations, creams, powders, and

blushes. Dawn pulls out both trays and begins her first self-beautification process. She begins to put on the makeup in the same order she remembers the attendants at the spa using. She completes the makeup job and is confident she has done well. She admires herself in the mirror at length while fluffing her hair for faster drying. She opens the first drawer on the left side of the table to find brushes, combs, and picks. The next drawer has a blow dryer and some curling irons. She pulls out the dryer and one of the larger curling irons. She plugs the dryer and the iron into plugs located at the bottom of the mirror. She begins to blow dry her hair, while the curling iron heats up. As her hair dries, the natural curl becomes wavy. After she is done with the blow dryer, she uses a wide-toothed pick to loosen tangles created by the dryer. Starting at the back, she begins to twirl strands of hair around the curling iron. When her entire head has been twirled into curls, she runs the pick through her hair to give height and waviness to her hairdo. Completely satisfied with her hair, Dawn sprays some finishing lacquer, she found in the bottom drawer, on it. She wheels herself back a little from the mirror to get a better look at the entire finished product.

"I look great," Dawn says to herself, "Even if I do say so myself."

She gets up from the table and exits the bathroom. She walks over to the bureau containing the tray of fragrances. She sprays a small mist from several bottles and sniffs to find one she likes best. She selects one and generously sprays around her hair and neck and down her arms. As she replaces the bottle to the tray, she sees her necklace draping over the edge of the mirror above the bureau. She removes it and places it around her neck. The blue of the sweater turns the yellow stone green as it reflects through. Dawn opens one of the curtains to allow the sunlight to spread across the floor and over the bed. She holds the necklace up to her eye and looks through the stone into the sunlight. She has a perfectly clear view of the window. She moves closer to see outside. She can see a pathway and trees almost at arms-length away. She lowers the necklace to see the pathway and trees with the naked eye. She can barely make out anything through the window. The stone apparently has magnification properties that make things appear closer. She looks again at the pathway and trees through the stone. Fascinated by the necklace, she takes a moment to examine it closer. Hearing her stomach rumble, Dawn decides it's time for breakfast. She drops the necklace and watches it fall down her chest bouncing against her belly just below her breasts. She makes her way to the door, looks around the room to make sure she hasn't forgotten anything, opens the door, and exits.

She stands outside the room for a moment and looks over the banister to see the foyer below. She reaches out to touch the banister as she walks along the hallway to the staircase. Feeling rested and refreshed, she bounces down the staircase. At the bottom she turns to walk in the direction, she believes, is the dining room or kitchen. No sooner has she walked but a few steps than Bessie comes running down the wide hallway and nuzzles around Dawn's feet. Dawn reaches down and picks her up.

"Oh, Bessie," Dawn says as she kisses her on the head, "Where have you been?"

Still toting Bessie in her arms, Dawn continues down the hallway. About halfway down, she sees Ida coming from a room off to the right.

"Good morning, Miss Hunter," Ida says, "I'll bet you're hungry."

"Yes, I am," Dawn replies.

Ida takes Bessie and directs Dawn towards the room she just exited. Ida turns to the left and places Bessie into another room. Dawn turns right and enters the room pointed out by Ida. It is obviously a dining room but a small one. Aunt Eva is seated in her wheelchair at the opposite end. James is seated at her right, and Ms. Johnson is seated at her left. There is room at the table for three more people. Aunt Eva motions for her to come in and be seated by James. As she approaches the table, she sees a large tray of fruit on a 'Lazy Susan' in the middle of the table. She sits down in front of a place setting next to James. No sooner does she sit than another servant brings a plate of eggs, bacon, potatoes, and pancakes and places it in front of her.

"Would you like tea?" the servant asks Dawn.

"No, thank you, just orange juice," Dawn replies.

While Dawn fidgets to place the cloth napkin on her lap, Aunt Eva begins her morning greeting.

"How are you today, my dear?" Aunt Eva asks, "Did you sleep well? You really had a full day yesterday, and I hope you are not too tired. There are a few things you need to do today. After I fill you in on the estate and your responsibilities for it, you will be spending the afternoon with Xavier."

"My responsibilities?" Dawn says as she looks up in puzzlement.

"Yes, my dear," Aunt Eva replies, "This estate is yours. It belonged to your mother and now it's yours."

Dawn almost chokes on the forkful of potatoes she just put in her mouth.

"The whole estate?" she inquires after swallowing the contents of her mouth, "What about you and Uncle George? Shouldn't it belong to you?"

"I have another estate just west of here, and George has a smaller estate down south," Aunt Eva explains, "These are all family estates that we all share, but each of us has an estate to take care of. This one is yours. All the servants, caretakers, and chauffeurs are under your direction."

"Oh, wow," Dawn exclaims, "I don't know much about directing."

"Everyone here knows their job and needs little direction," Aunt Eva continues, "But they need to know you are 'in charge' and can make decisions for those extraordinary situations."

"Well, I'm not sure about that," Dawn replies, "But I will do my best to be 'in charge.' How tough can it be?"

With that, she goes back to eating her breakfast.

"What time is Zac coming over?" Dawn inquires.

"He should be here any minute for breakfast," Ms. Johnson says.

"Yes," Aunt Eva continues, "He will be getting the workout room ready while you, I, and James finish our conversation we began

last night. So, after you finish breakfast,
return to your room and get the book. Ida
will escort you back to the tech lab. Just
buzz her from your room when you are ready."

Just then, the door leading to the
outside opens and in walks Zac.

"Good morning, everyone," he joyfully
says with a wide smile, "It's a beautiful
day."

Dawn looks up and catches Zac bending
over to kiss Aunt Eva on the cheek.

"How's my favorite girl?" he continues.

Zac glances at Dawn and winks as he makes
his way to the place setting next to Ms.
Johnson, just across from Dawn. Dawn smiles
to indicate her flattery at the small,
flirtatious gesture. No sooner has he sat
down than the same servant brings him a plate
full of breakfast.

"Would you like tea?" the servant asks.

"Why, yes, please," Zac replies
graciously.

The servant proceeds to pour tea into a
cup in front of Zac as he reaches for the
cream and sugar to 'doctor up' his tea. He
places his napkin in his lap and most
vigorously begins eating the contents of the
plate. He looks up occasionally to find Dawn
staring at him between bites of her own
breakfast. He thinks she is enamored with his
good looks, but in reality she is enamored
with his obviously healthy appetite.

Finished with her breakfast and morning
tea, Aunt Eva begins outlining the plan for
the day.

"Ms. Johnson," she begins, "Will you go
to the study. There is some correspondence
that needs to be opened and evaluated. There
are some bills that need attention. I will

take care of them until Dawn is in a position to take care of them herself. Will you also prepare the necessary paperwork for Dawn to write checks and oversee the banking requirements. She will also need a credit card."

Ms. Johnson nods; and having completed her breakfast, she excuses herself from the table and heads to the study.

"Xavier," Aunt Eva continues, "You need to prepare the workout room for Dawn's session this afternoon. But, take your time. Dawn, James, and I have some business in the tech lab this morning. I'm not sure how long it will take, but there will definitely be enough time for you to show Dawn 'the ropes.'"

Dawn appears to be a little puzzled. What kind of 'workout' does Aunt Eva think she needs? Just as she is about to ask, Zac responds to Aunt Eva's direction.

"Yes, ma'am," Zac says playfully, "I will get the ropes ready to show Miss Hunter."

Aunt Eva giggles at the pun Zac has made in reference to a workout with ropes. Again, he winks at Dawn as he looks over at her. Aunt Eva excuses herself as James begins to wheel her from the room to the hallway. With Zac being the only one left to finish his breakfast, Dawn smiles at him and follows James and Aunt Eva into the hallway. James pushes Aunt Eva down another hallway as Dawn proceeds back to her room.

As Dawn approaches the room where Ida had taken Bessie, she decides she wants to make sure Bessie is comfortable. She opens the door to a large, well-lit room. She shuts the door behind her as she notices Bessie stretched out on a long settee. Dawn looks over at a table on the opposite side of the room where Angus is chirping happily and swinging from his perch. Under the table are two bowls; one for water and one for food. At the far end of the room, Dawn can see a large, kitty-litter box. Dawn meanders over to the settee and sits next to Bessie. Dawn vigorously rubs her belly as she remains all stretched out.

"Well, Bessie-Boo," Dawn says, "I certainly don't have to worry about you. You have made yourself at home here and very comfortably, I might add."

Dawn gets up from the settee and walks over to Angus' cage. She sticks her finger through one of the bars of the cage to gently stroke his feathers. Not being able to reach him, Dawn just mouths him a kiss and heads back to the door. She exits the room and continues her way back to her own bedroom.

As she enters her room, she formulates a plan to extract the book from the bag hidden between the two mattresses of her bed. She tries to lift the top mattress to expose the bag. It was easier putting it there than getting it out. Not being able to lift the mattress high enough to see the bag, Dawn wiggles her arms under the top mattress, back and forth. Her fingers catch on one of the straps. She tries to slowly pull on the strap so as not to lose her grip of it. Gradually, Dawn inches the bag out from under the mattress. She places in on top of the bed for easier access. She unzips it and reaches in to retrieve the brown, leather book. With book in hand, she leaves the bedroom and heads to the tech lab.

CHAPTER SIXTEEN

Not knowing whether Ida is trustworthy, Dawn decides to find the tech lab by herself. She makes her way up the wide hallway, into a smaller hallway, and up three flights of stairs until she reaches the familiar door with a buzzer on the wall. She pushes the buzzer and waits until James appears in the window. He opens the door for her and looks around to see that Ida did not accompany her this time.

"You're getting much acquainted with your surroundings," James says as he closes the door behind her and circles around to open the next door.

Dawn walks through the next door, over the cords and cables, and around the tables to the main desk with the wall monitor. She places the book on the desk in front of Aunt Eva who is looking at some dark splotches on another graph displayed on the monitor. James seats himself in the chair next to Aunt Eva.

"Do you know what these splotches are?" Aunt Eva asks Dawn as she turns to get a better look at her.

"No," Dawn replies, "But, there are a lot of them."

"They are body heat indicators," Aunt Eva states.

"Whose body heat?" Dawn asks.

"Well, let me finish my story," Aunt Eva says, "After our father died, George and I had limited magical powers. We wanted to monitor the hedge where the old witch had been imprisoned, but we didn't dare use even the slightest amount of magic anywhere near the hedge. So, James, being a very smart tech geek, suggested we use high-tech computer

networking to monitor the hedge. He laid out
a grid of the hedge and strategically placed
wiring and sensors all around to capture body
heat and electrical charges created by
performing magic, which we suspected the witch
would do to survive in the hedge. With the
help of the local electric company, we placed
long electric poles along the outer edges of
the hedge and ran wires and sensors across the
top of the hedge bracing them around the poles
at each end. Using network language
programming, James was able to configure the
sensors to detect body heat and electric
charges. For the past several years, James
has been running scan after scan to record any
activity reflective of body heat and
electricity. You ask, 'Whose body heat?'
Well, we believe the witch has built an army
of soldiers using magic to turn squirrels and
other vermin into men. That's what all the
splotches mean."

"When we first discovered the splotches,"
James continues, "We recorded all the activity
very carefully. Based on patterns and
frequency of movement as well as periodic
additions of splotches, we concluded that men
were being formed to protect the witch.
Squirrels and vermin would not generate enough
heat to form a splotch of this size on the
grid. And, as you said, there are a lot of
them. So, her army is becoming substantial."

Surprisingly, Dawn totally understands
everything James and Aunt Eva has just told
her.

"What about the blinking light you found
yesterday?" Dawn asks James.

"Well," Aunt Eva begins, "Over a month
ago, one of the sensors at the far end of the
hedge began to flicker. James was afraid it

might burst. Not knowing what kind of spell Hilda used to encase the hedge, we didn't want to take a chance that a blown sensor would impact the spell in any way. Magical spells are somewhat dynamic in nature. We didn't have enough magical powers at hand to counteract any intrusion of the spell from outside sources. So, James had George take the 'cherry picker' to the location of the bad sensor and try to replace it. He was able to replace the sensor but accidentally fell into the hedge. He disappeared and hasn't been seen or heard from since. He apparently fell through a portal which we can't find or see, and he can't get out through the portal if he can't see it either. He was wearing an 'ear bug' but doesn't respond when we try to contact him. The blinking light is a transmission from the 'ear bug.' The signal isn't moving, and it is very faint."

"So, what are you saying?" Dawn asks, "Is Uncle George dead?"

"Well, we're not sure," James replies, "He could be hiding or he may have lost the 'ear bug.' So far, the splotches are not in the vicinity of the blinking light. So George may be safe if he is hiding. However, if he is one of the splotches, he may be a prisoner of the witch."

"Wouldn't you see a splotch closer to the blinking light if George was hiding?" Dawn inquires.

Realizing Dawn may be sharper than he expected, James tries to provide an explanation.

"We don't know what kind of objects are in the hedge," James says, "If George is hiding under something metal or something that will deflect sensor detection, he won't

126

manifest on the grid. That, too, may explain the faintness of the 'ear bug' signal. His head may be exposed just enough to capture the 'ear bug' signal but not the heat from his entire body."

Dawn now has a suspicious notion that all this is being shared with her for a particular reason. Not because she is the new owner of the estate on which the hedge is located, but because Aunt Eva expects her to magically do something to find Uncle George and kill the witch and her army at the same time. Just over a week ago, Dawn lived a dull, humdrum life. Her only worries were feeding her cat and bird and going to work. A far cry from performing magic and fulfilling a family legacy. Dawn only hopes the book will have enough information and answers to make her feel confident she is worthy and capable to fulfill this prophecy Aunt Eva has placed at her feet.

"Your mother predicted you would be the one," Aunt Eva says as she pulls a folded piece of paper from her pocket, "After I sent a letter to your mother a month before she died, I received this back from her."

Aunt Eva hands the paper to Dawn. Dawn unfolds it and begins to read out loud.

"Morning seeker with powers abound,
The portal entrance will be found.
Only the seeker can open gates,
And overturn the family fates.
Evening sky oversees the plan,
To end the curse and save the clan."

"What the heck does this mean?" Dawn asks somewhat puzzled, "I thought I knew my own mother. Now, I find out she was a witch, and she wrote poetry."

"This means," Aunt Eva tries to explain, "That you are our savior. Morning seeker is Dawn Hunter. You know, morning — dawn, seeker — hunter. That's you. Evening sky, that's me. My married name is Eva Ninsky. Your mother thought Eva Ninsky sounded like evening sky, so she would always call me 'evening sky.' Her letter is a prediction that you will enter the hedge through the portal and kill the witch and her army. I will help from the outside using all the technology we have available. Unfortunately, your mother didn't know that George would fall into the hedge and require rescuing. That will be an added glitch to your journey."

"Let me get this straight," Dawn begins to laugh and says sarcastically, "You expect me to enter the hedge through some portal, kill a witch and her entire army, and find and rescue Uncle George. Then, exit the hedge through the same portal with Uncle George. Have I got that right?"

"Well, yes," Aunt Eva replies, "It sounds much easier when you say it. However, it's not going to be a piece of crumpet."

"You mean a piece of cake, don't you," Dawn replies.

Dawn takes her mother's letter, folds it back up, and places it into the pocket of her slacks. She begins to walk around the small area in front of the wall monitor. She presses her fingers against her temples as if to relieve some pressure she is sure is the cause of a pending headache. It couldn't be the drastic unveiling of pending doom thrown upon her in the last two days.

"Okay," Dawn says as she realizes that she can't just walk away, "I need to know what's in that book. It is locked, so we need to find the three-digit code. I've already tried the most obvious combinations. Mother's birthday; my birthday. They didn't work. What could the code be?"

"I will have James run some computer-generated, combination-sequence possibilities," Aunt Eva replies, "We will work on that the rest of the afternoon. The book will be safe here. It is now twelve-thirty. You need to meet with Zac in the workout room for your lesson. Besides learning magic, you will need to be prepared physically. Zac will teach you weaponry; how to use a sword, a bow and arrow, and a pistol. Because the witch has magic, too, you will need another edge. Weaponry will be your advantage. We haven't much time left, so learn what you can. Your mother would not have predicted your involvement in this if she didn't think you would succeed. She knew something about you that you don't know about yourself. She will be with you."

"I certainly hope so," Dawn says, "I have a bone to pick with her. If she knows something about me that I don't, I hope she will share it with me before I get myself killed or turned into a dragon."

Aunt Eva smiles and motions to Dawn to move on to the workout room where Zac is undoubtedly waiting.

"By the way," Dawn inquires, "Does Zac know anything about all this? Does he know what he's preparing me for?"

"Yes," Aunt Eva replies, "He knows. His mother and father were very good friends of my mother and father. They, too, dabbled in magic but chose to cease the practice when my father did. Xavier is not the first born, so his magical powers are as limited as mine. He was very small when your mother left England but has been informed over the years of the spell she cast before she left and the legacy that haunts our family."

As Dawn makes her way to the door, James follows to make sure both doors close behind her. Dawn descends the three levels of stairs and walks through the narrow hallway into the wider hallway. Now, to find the workout room.

Dawn turns left down the wider hallway just as Ida is visible at the opposite end. Dawn maintains her customary pace while Ida walks rather briskly to stop Dawn from traveling too far down the hallway.

"The workout room is this way," Ida advises as she turns down another hallway.

Dawn follows, picking up her pace in order to keep up with Ida. At the end of this hallway, there are double glass doors leading to the outside. Ida opens a large, wooden door in the middle of the hallway and waits as Dawn passes her and takes a moment to look outside through the glass doors. When Dawn returns, she follows Ida into a large room.

One side of the room is nothing but glass windows with a glass French door in the middle which obviously opens outside to another small patio and large, lawn area. There are long, thick ropes hanging from the ceiling in the corner and targets strategically located against the opposite wall. There are mannequins standing in the middle of the floor that appear to have been battered with clubs or swords or whatever. Dawn can't quite decide what kind of weapon would make marks like that. Just as she is about to get a closer look at the damages, Zac comes into the room from a small door at the opposite end. As he approaches Dawn, Ida decides her services are no longer required; so she makes her way out.

"Are you ready for your workout?" Zac says as he reaches out for Dawn's hand.

"I'm not sure I know, at this point, what I'm ready for," Dawn replies.

Dawn has had to process a 'grundel' of information in the last two days. Some of it not very pleasant, and some of it totally unbelievable. Zac can see that this newfound responsibility is weighing heavy on her. Exposing her to swords, bows, arrows, and guns right now may not be particularly beneficial. Still holding her hand, he begins to walk towards the French doors as Dawn follows.

CHAPTER SEVENTEEN

Once outside, Dawn takes in a deep breath of fresh air. She is hoping that will clear her mind enough to make room for any other new developments she will be required to stuff in her head. Zac lets go of her hand and quickly walks to a small shed attached to the house at the end of the patio. He opens the door and steps inside. He has disappeared from Dawn's view, so she begins to walk towards the shed when she hears the revving of a motor. Straddling a four-wheeled ATV, Zac backs out of the shed and maneuvers his way in front of Dawn. He slides up as far as he can to make room for Dawn on the back. He reaches out his arm to assist her in mounting the vehicle. Once comfortably settled, Dawn wraps her arms around Zac's waist as he presses the accelerator with his thumb to generate forward movement. Off they go; across the large, green lawn. From the side of the house, they travel as far west as they can until they run out of lawn. Then, Zac makes a ninety-degree turn traveling north. Dawn looks around at the trees and bushes that almost hide the tall, brick wall that apparently borders the entire estate. When they reach what appears to be the end, Dawn can see a very tall hedge that runs another ninety degrees from the brick wall.

"This is the beginning of the famous hedge," Zac says, "It extends along the back side of the entire estate. The river is on the other side of it."

Zac turns the ATV to run parallel with the hedge and accelerates enough for Dawn to get a 'bird's eye' view of the hedge. Dawn can see the house past another large patch of lawn and a rose garden to the south as they travel east. As the house disappears behind them, Zac abruptly stops in front of another brick wall.

"This is the end of the hedge," he says, "My family estate is just over this wall. We can get to the river from there, but you can't get to it from here."

Dawn flips her leg over Zac, slides off the ATV, and walks towards the hedge. It looks like any other hedge; maybe somewhat larger. She reaches out to touch the hedge and feels a tingling sensation in her fingertips as she inches closer. Her hand abruptly stops any further, forward motion; but Dawn can't see anything that would obstruct her hand from reaching completely through the large leaves. It is a weird feeling, like trying to run but finding your feet won't move.

Zac dismounts the ATV but leans against it while he watches Dawn try to figure out the mystery of the hedge. She moves back and forth for about ten feet trying to poke her hand into the leaves but to no avail. She returns to the ATV where Zac pulls her in close and puts his arms around her waist. He bends down to kiss her. His soft lips send shivers down her spine. She can't help grabbing his face and kissing him back. For the first time since she arrived, Dawn is experiencing something real, something wonderful. She hopes this moment will go on forever. But, even good things must end.

As they pull apart, Dawn stares deep into Zac's dark brown eyes. He smiles, flings his leg over the ATV, and takes Dawn's hand to help her once again mount the vehicle. He starts the motor and backs the ATV away from the brick wall. He turns sharply and begins to accelerate just enough to prolong the journey back to the house. When they arrive back at the shed, Chumley is waiting on the patio.

"Would you like lunch out here on the patio, miss?" Chumley asks.

Dawn is still hanging tightly to Zac. She is trying to take in as much closeness as she can. Her mind is clear, and she feels so relaxed. She sees Chumley, but doesn't hear a word he says. Zac turns off the ATV motor as Chumley approaches the vehicle.

"Would you like lunch out here on the patio, miss?" Chumley asks again.

Dawn makes eye contact with Chumley as she slides off the ATV. She walks around to the front of the vehicle and glances at Zac.

"Does my workout include lunch?" she asks with a smile, "I have really worked up an appetite."

"Yes, these workouts do tend to make one hungry," Zac says sarcastically.

"Well, then, lunch on the patio," Dawn says to Chumley.

"Very good, miss," Chumley responds as he walks back into the workout room through the French doors.

Zac starts up the motor of the ATV again and drives it back into the shed. He closes the shed door and walks back onto the patio where he left Dawn. He grabs her hand and pulls it in close to this chest. He turns to face Dawn in an attempt to steal another kiss; however, his plan is thwarted by the arrival of Ida pushing a cart across the patio towards the picnic table. Realizing she has interrupted a romantic moment, Ida blushes and moves even more quickly towards the table.

Dawn and Zac giggle as they follow her a
little more slowly.

As they situate themselves next to each
other at the table, Ida arranges two place
settings. After she has completed arrangement
of the food trays, Dawn looks at Zac to
indicate her surprise at the abundance of food
prepared just for lunch. Ida approaches Dawn
to assist in filling her beverage glass.

"I think we can take it from here, Ida,"
Dawn assures her, "Thanks so much."

Zac nods to indicate he, too, is capable
of filling his own glass. They both sit back
and watch as Ida briskly walks back across the
patio and into the French doors.

As Dawn reaches across the table to
access the trays, she fills her plate with a
variety of fruits, salads, and sandwiches.
She notices that Zac is not one bit bashful as
he fills his plate with food from the trays.
As a matter of fact, they both seem to be very
comfortable with each other. Dawn wants to
think that the kiss may have broken the ice.
She certainly doesn't need any more tension in
her life. It is refreshing to think she might
have an ally in all this, a very attractive
and romantic ally at that.

After she swallows a mouthful of salad,
Dawn decides it's time to 'cash in' on this
new alliance, "Aunt Eva told me that you are
aware of our family legacy and the
unbelievable story of a witch that threatens
our future."

"Yes, I am," Zac says with a sandwich in
hand, "But, my family is part of that legacy
as well. My mother and father have magical
powers, too. When your grandfather decided
that magic was too dangerous to use and
started to destroy any proof of its existence,

my mother and father joined forces with him to eliminate not only the use of magic but also the need for it. Your grandmother secretly defied your grandfather and covertly practiced magic. My mother and father rallied with your grandfather when the witch cast the spell that killed your grandmother. As a result, the witch threatened to destroy my family as well. So, you see, I have a vested interest in making sure the witch doesn't leave that hedge alive."

Dawn takes a deep breath and sighs in relief. She now realizes that she is not in this alone. To have an ally with a vested interest is even better than just a friend helping out. With a renewed confidence, Dawn feels she can now conquer anything. She's not afraid of some old witch. Just as she is about to take another forkful of salad, Zac leans over and kisses her.

"We are in this together," Zac assures her as he stares intently into her piercing blue eyes.

Dawn smiles at him and gives his hand a gentle squeeze indicating her relief.

"Now," he says, "We didn't get much done today, but we will hit it hard tomorrow."

"Well," Dawn replies, "That will certainly give me something to look forward to. And, if a kiss is my reward for doing well, I will undoubtedly be at my best."

Dawn giggles as she leans over to kiss him. This kiss is a little more meaningful and passionate. It lasts a lot longer, too. The sound of someone moving across the patio interferes with the romantic moment. Both Dawn and Zac straighten up in their chairs. Dawn looks around to see Ida walking towards them.

"Your aunt is asking for you, miss," Ida says.

"Is she still in the tech lab?" Dawn inquires.

"Yes, she is," Ida replies.

"Maybe she has found a hint to the combination of the book," Dawn says to Zac after Ida makes her way back across the patio.

"The book?" Zac inquires.

Dawn tells Zac the story of her mother going to the United States with the book, "Apparently, my grandmother had hidden the book from my grandfather when he was destroying all evidence of magic. She and my mother would practice magic regularly in the basement using this book for direction. After the witch cast her spell and my grandfather sent my mother to the United States for her safety, my mother took the book with her unbeknownst to my grandfather. Aunt Eva knew about the book and told me to bring it with me to England. It is apparently going to help me revive any magical powers I may have as the first born. Aunt Eva says the secrets of magic are in the book."

"Sounds like we have a cushion in our quest to kill the witch," Zac says, "If you can hone your magical powers using this book, we will stand a much better chance."

Dawn likes the sound of 'we.' She feels much more relaxed knowing she has a partner. The absurdity of this venture seems less unachievable. She feels like she can conquer the world; however, conquering the world may be much easier than killing a witch and her army and rescuing Uncle George while trying to find an entrance and exit in a large hedge enclosed in an unidentifiable barrier. It all sounds so complicated.

Both Dawn and Zac arise from the table at the same time. Zac grabs Dawn's hand as they walk slowly across the patio. Once inside the workout room, Zac begins to outline the plan for them for tomorrow while walking Dawn to the door leading to the hallway.

"I will be back in the morning for breakfast," Zac says, "We will get an early start on your physical training. I'm sure Aunt Eva will outline the plan for your magical training after you have accessed the book. So, good luck; and I'll see you tomorrow."

Zac kisses her on the hand and makes his way across the workout room and disappears behind another door. Dawn exits the room into the hallway. Knowing this is not the hallway leading to the tech lab, Dawn backtracks to the main hallway. Walking down the wide hallway, she recognizes the next hallway as being the right one. She turns into this hallway, up three flights of stairs, and ends up in front of the door with the window. She pushes the buzzer and waits until James appears in the window. As before, Dawn makes her way through both doors, over the cords and cables, and around to where Aunt Eva is waiting with a piece of paper in her hand.

"James has run a special program identifying all possible sequences for a three-digit code," Aunt Eva reports, "All we have to do now is look at them to see if there is anything that looks familiar or would logically be the right code."

Dawn begins to fidget with her necklace in anticipation of determining what the three-digit code could possibly be. As she runs her fingers across the back of the necklace, she feels the indentions. She quickly switches her attention to the back of the necklace. She pulls the necklace closer to her face to get a better look at the indentions. Remembering there are three of them, she is now wondering if those indentions have anything to do with the three-digit code. She thinks it is too coincidental not to have some significance.

"Aunt Eva," Dawn begins, "This necklace has three indentions on the back. They are very small and unreadable with the naked eye. Do you think they might be the three-digit code needed to open the book?"

Aunt Eva opens a drawer underneath the computer table and pulls out a magnifying glass. She reaches out as Dawn bends over enough for her to grasp the necklace. She turns the necklace over and begins to inspect it through the magnifying glass.

"I see an 'A' and a 'V' and an 'E,'" Aunt Eva reports.

"Those are letters," Dawn says, "We need numbers."

"AVE," James repeats, "Maybe it should be EVA. Maybe this is your necklace, Eva."

"No," Aunt Eva replies, "Our mother was very specific. Hilda got the yellow stone because she reminded her of the brightness of the day. I got the dark blue stone because I reminded her of the blue sky of night."

Looking a little perplexed, Dawn is mulling something around in her mind. She shares something that occurs to her, "Maybe this is a message to refer to your necklace, Aunt Eva."

Aunt Eva lifts her wrist to her mouth, pushes one of the buttons, and begins to talk, "Ida, will you bring my small, red, jewelry box from my room up to the tech lab."

"Yes, ma'am," Ida's voice echoes back through a small speaker in Aunt Eva's bracelet.

Aunt Eva smiles broadly at Dawn as if she had just won the lottery, "You have your mother's intellect. That will serve you well in your upcoming endeavor."

Dawn begins to pace around the tables waiting for the sound of the buzzer. Not having to wait too long, James makes his way to the door in response to the buzzer. James returns with the red, jewelry box and places it in the waiting hands of Aunt Eva. She opens the box and pulls out a blue, satin pouch. She pulls her necklace from the pouch and places the pouch and box on the nearest table. She grabs the magnifying glass and begins to examine the back of her necklace. Eureka! She finds three indentions of numbers.

"Write these numbers down, James," Aunt Eva directs.

While waiting for James to get a piece of paper and pen, Aunt Eva looks up at Dawn with a very satisfying expression and winks. Seeing that James is ready to record her findings, she begins to recite the numbers, "Eight, three, zero."

After she is sure James has written the numbers correctly, Aunt Eva places her necklace in her lap and reaches out to retrieve the paper with the numbers. She looks at them intently.

"We need to only determine the order of the numbers," Aunt Eva says.

"Maybe the order is the same as 'EVA' would be on my necklace," Dawn says.

"Brilliant," Aunt Eva says loudly.

Dawn moves closer to Aunt Eva so she can look at her necklace again. She examines Dawn's necklace and evaluates the order of the letters. She transfers that order mentally onto her necklace to coincide with the numbers.

"The sequence should be 'three, zero, eight,'" Aunt Eva says.

James takes the paper from Aunt Eva and writes down the new sequence of numbers crossing off the first set of numbers. He walks around some tables and stands in front of a picture of 'dogs playing cards.' He pushes a small button at the bottom of the picture frame and waits while the picture rises straight up. When the picture stops rising, Dawn can see a safe door hidden behind the picture. James begins to turn the knob, back and forth. When he completes the combination sequence, he moves the long lever downward and opens the safe door. Inside is the brown, leather book. He pulls it from the safe and places it on the desk in front of Aunt Eva. Aunt Eva turns the book sideways to get a better look at the combination clasp. As Dawn and James looks over each shoulder, Aunt Eva begins to move the first tumbler. She moves it down until the number '3' is visible, then the next tumbler to the number '0.' She pulls her hands away from the book and looks around at Dawn and James.

"This is it," she says, "The moment of truth."

She moves the last tumbler to number '8.' No sooner does she take her hands away than the clasp opens. Aunt Eva sits back in her chair again, and all three of them just stare at the book. Aunt Eva makes the first move towards the book. She turns it back around so she can open it from right to left making it visible for Dawn and James. She turns the brown, leather book cover to expose the first page. All three bend over the book to get a better look. The writing is somewhat foreign. Aunt Eva touches the first page to turn it and finds it to be very fragile. So, she uses her other hand to cradle it so as not to tear or damage it. Without taking the time to read and interpret the writing, Aunt Eva proceeds to turn pages.

It is apparent that these writings are very old, and it is obvious this book has been handed down from generation to generation. The initial writings may be so old they will not be recognizable in this modern day. However, Aunt Eva and Dawn are hopeful they will be able to make sense of them.

As Aunt Eva continues to thumb through the pages, she points out brief sections of rhythmic chants and, what looks like, recipes. She begins to turn several pages at a time until she reaches the end. She turns the back cover over to completely close the book.

"It's getting late," Aunt Eva says, "Let's get a good night's sleep and delve into the book tomorrow. I know Xavier is coming in the morning for breakfast and will begin the physical training right after. James plans to run several scans in the morning to record movement activity in the hedge. We need to analyze the scans to see if we can determine a pattern that will be helpful once you penetrate the hedge. If we can find the portal that provides an entrance and exit point, we will be able to outline a 'plan of attack,' so to speak."

Aunt Eva picks up the book and hands it to James. He proceeds to take it back to the safe. After he closes the safe and waits until the picture has returned to its place in front, he motions for Dawn to follow him to the door. Once again, she makes her way down the stairs, into both hallways, up her own staircase, and into her bedroom. It's been a full day, and she is very tired. She changes into her pajamas, washes her face, brushes her teeth, and jumps into bed.

CHAPTER EIGHTEEN

Dawn begins to toss and turn. Her eyes are closed, and she feels very tired; but she just can't seem to relax. After several minutes, she sits up and opens her eyes. She looks groggily around the room in hopes of finding her eyes will become heavy, weary, and longing for more sleep.

But instead she sees an image walking towards her. At first she thinks it must be Ida coming to wake her up; but as the image gets closer, she recognizes it as her mother. She covers her eyes with her hands in an attempt to convince herself she is seeing things. She takes her hands away from her eyes only to witness her mother at the side of her bed.

"My dear, Dawn," her mother says as she sits on the edge of the bed, "I am so sorry I wasn't able to properly prepare you for this endeavor. It was supposed to be mine. I wanted to protect you from the dangers resulting from our family legacy. However, knowing you possess great magical powers, I have provided written guidance in the last section of the book to assist with your journey. All the information and guidance in the book is invaluable and includes writings from many generations of our family; but I have specifically addressed spells that will help conquer the witch in the hedge, since it was my spell that put her there. You will be triumphant, and I will be with you in heart and mind."

Not being able to say a word, Dawn watches as her mother drifts back into the darkness and disappears. She just sits and ponders what her mother told her. After several moments, she takes a deep breath, lays her head back down on the pillow, and falls asleep.

Once again, Dawn wakes up without the assistance of any outside source. No maid, no alarm, no Bessie or Angus. After the day she had yesterday, she is surprisingly rested. Then she gets this gnawing sensation that she should be remembering something. What is it? Immediately, thoughts of her mother come to the forefront of her mind. That's it! She remembers dreaming about her mother. She now recalls the reality of it; but knowing her mother is dead, she realizes it had to be a dream. But, it felt so real.

Dawn gets out of bed and quickly transfers her thoughts to Zac. She knows he is going to be the backbone of her success. Not knowing the extent of her magical powers, she is sure she will be depending a lot on him which sounds rather 'yummy.' Dawn licks her lips at just the thought.

She looks at the clock. It is almost eight o'clock. She tries to quickly formulate a plan in her head, so she will be prompt for the breakfast table and ready for her training session thereafter. She knows she will shower, do her hair and makeup, and dress appropriately for a promising workout. Remembering the type of attire that Zac was wearing yesterday, she goes to her closet to find an outfit that is equal to the one he was wearing. He had on some black pants with a matching, long-sleeved shirt and black, military-style boots. The fabric of the shirt and pants were different than anything she had felt or seen before.

She rifles through her closet to see if she can find anything that feels the same.

She stops at a section where she is sure the fabric on this hangar is similar, if not exact, to the fabric Zac was wearing. It is a long-sleeved, black shirt and, next to it, is a pair of pants. She takes them both from the closet and lays them on the bed. The pants are not tight fitting, so she thinks she will wear a pair of black tights under the pants to avoid wearing bulky socks. She goes to her shoe closet to find her own black, military-style boots. Finding the same outfit in her closet that Zac was wearing, she is sure she will also find the boots. Sure enough, there they are. Too big to fit on the shoe rack, Dawn finds them on a shelf to the side of the rack. She pulls them out and sets them on the floor next to the bed. She goes to the bureau to find black tights. Now that all her apparel is neatly placed on her bed, she is ready for her shower.

After she gets dressed and does her makeup, Dawn decides to just blow dry her hair and wear it in a ponytail, keeping her hair from getting tangled during her training. Ready for the day, she exits her bedroom and heads down the hall and stairs towards the small dining room. She enters the dining room only to find Ms. Johnson seated at the table.

"Well," Ms. Johnson says as she looks up at Dawn, "Looks like you are ready for your training session."

Dawn hasn't had much time to spend with Ms. Johnson since they arrived at the estate. Dawn felt a certain closeness develop when they were at the hotel in London. Ms. Johnson seems to be a little more distant now.

"How are you today, Nancy?" Dawn asks as she seats herself across the table.

146

She deliberately calls her 'Nancy' to project a friendly tone to her question and to let her know she is not forgotten.

"I am fine, Dawn," Ms. Johnson responds, "It is good to see you getting 'on board' with everything around here. I want you to know you can depend on me to help run the estate while you are getting your feet wet."

"Thank you, Nancy," Dawn replies, "I don't want to shirk my responsibilities, but I'm sure I will need as much help as I can get. I'm finding there are many things I won't be doing alone."

Ms. Johnson looks puzzled at the comment but doesn't pursue an explanation. Dawn wasn't about to elaborate anyway, so the conversation just sort of fizzled. And in the nick of time, too! A servant enters the dining room with a plate of breakfast for Dawn. Today, it is Belgian waffles and fruit with a side of ham. Just as Dawn takes her napkin from the table and places it in her lap, the outside door opens. Zac bounces in and, instead of seating himself next to Ms. Johnson, walks around the table to sit by Dawn.

"Good morning, ladies," Zac says with a smile.

Ms. Johnson mumbles something resembling 'good morning' but realizes she is being ignored as Zac begins admiring Dawn's breakfast.

"I'm starving," he says, "I had a late lunch yesterday and no dinner."

"Oh, you poor darling," Dawn responds, "We can't have our growing boy starving. Can we, Nancy?"

Ms. Johnson looks up from her breakfast to see if Dawn really expects an answer. Of course not. Dawn is sheepishly staring at Zac as if they are the only ones in the room. Zac is trying to steal some of Dawn's fruit but changes his plan when he sees the servant enter the room with his breakfast. Dawn looks around the room to see if she can spot cameras or surveillance equipment of any kind. She is always amazed that the people around here seem to know when someone arrives, where they are, and when they leave. She feels good knowing there is a high level of security, but she hopes that the security will not infringe on her privacy.

Now that Zac has a plate of his own, Dawn begins to delve into her own Belgian waffles. As she is about to put a large forkful into her mouth, she sees Aunt Eva and James enter the dining room. James pushes Aunt Eva to her place at the head of the table; and since Dawn has taken his usual place, he seats himself next to Ms. Johnson. Dawn begins to chew her waffles while making eye contact with Aunt Eva.

"I see you're ready for your training session, this morning, my dear," Aunt Eva says.

"Yes, I am," Dawn replies, "Zac took me around the estate property yesterday. It certainly is big."

Dawn doesn't dare say anything about the hedge not knowing who is privy to the family legacy. She is somewhat paranoid that someone might be listening outside the dining room. Her experience over the last few days has taught her that no one has ESP; they all wear 'ear bugs.' So, she will be careful what she says outside the tech lab.

"Well, as you know, you will be spending the morning with Xavier," Aunt Eva says to

Dawn, "And I will be spending it with Ms. Johnson. We will be taking care of some estate business that will be yours when you have time. James will be working in the tech lab and checking on some security issues outside. Our banker will be here at noon with some papers for you to sign. Once our bank business is done, we all will be meeting on the upper patio for lunch. After lunch, we have some more work to do in the tech lab. Xavier's mother and father are returning from London, and I have invited them here for dinner. I would like us all to be in the main dining room by five o'clock. Everyone knows the agenda for the day, so each carry on at their own pace. Xavier, before you begin your training session with Dawn, will you give her a quick tour of the inside of the house. Things have been moving along so quickly, we just haven't had the time to show her around. Also, James has an 'ear bug' for each of you. He will show you how to use them. Please get used to wearing them."

With that, Aunt Eva begins to eat her breakfast that was placed before her during her announcement of the plans for the day. Ms. Johnson makes 'small talk' with James, and Dawn and Zac are happily fighting over a piece of ham. Zac quickly eats the ham he won in the battle and washes it down with some orange juice. After getting their 'ear bugs' and instructions from James, Dawn and Zac leave the dining room and enter the wide hallway.

"I know where my room is," Dawn says as they inch their way to the middle of the hallway, "And the library and the tech lab and the workout room."

"Okay," Zac says as he takes her hand and heads towards the front of the house.

When they reach the front door, Zac points out her room at the top of the staircase, which she already knows, and then to the library on the other side of the foyer, which she also already knows. Still holding her hand, he leads her back down the wide hallway pointing to all the doors. He shows her the living room, the study, both dining rooms (small and main), the kitchen, and the laundry room, all down the wide hallway. Diverting to the smaller hallway, he points out the dance hall and the workout room. Taking another staircase Dawn has not seen before, he points out bedrooms and lavatories as they walk along a hallway that extends the entire length of the house. Except for the tech lab, Zac doesn't know what's on the third floor; so he bypasses it and takes Dawn to the roof. As he opens the door to the outside, Dawn can see across the flat surface to the edge of the house. The brick edging is about three feet high, undoubtedly used to keep people from falling from the roof.

Zac leads Dawn across the flat surface to the edge. As she looks over, she can see the hedge in the distance. With his arm around her neck, Zac points out all the other buildings; the garage, the boat house, the yard shed, the guest house, and several other buildings he isn't sure of. The servants' quarters are in the basement, but he doesn't bother taking her there. He just makes her aware of them.

"That concludes your tour, Miss Hunter," Zac says matter-of-factly, "Now, let's get down to the workout room and begin your training."

Dawn is a little surprised at his abruptness and his eagerness to get started on

her training. Her surprise doesn't last long
when she realizes that the 'ear bugs' have
taken away a certain amount of privacy. She
has to remember, others are listening. She
is, however, tempted to turn off her 'ear bug'
using the little control button attached to
her sleeve. But, she decides she needs to
evaluate the priority of things and put them
in perspective. She wants to tell him they
found the combination to the book and have
opened it, but she will pick another time to
avoid informing eavesdroppers. Zac closes and
locks the door to the roof, and they make
their way back down to the first level towards
the workout room.

CHAPTER NINETEEN

Inside the workout room, Zac immediately heads towards a large cupboard in the corner. He opens it and begins rummaging through dozens of swords. Dawn can hear the clanging as he tries to select one that doesn't outweigh her. He pulls one out and hands it to her. He goes back into the cupboard to find one for himself. While he is looking for his favorite, Dawn is swinging her sword up and around. She realizes she is not using the proper stance, because she moves off-balance with every swish. Almost falling over, she decides to wait for proper instructions.

Zac finds his sword, removes it from the rack, and shuts the cupboard door. With sword in hand, he motions Dawn to follow him to the area of the workout room where the mannequins are waiting for application of their intended purpose. Before practicing death blows on the mannequins, Zac gives Dawn instructions on how to stand for balance and techniques to establish proper circular motions of the weighted sword.

After an hour or so and being comfortable with her body movement and weapon skills, Dawn is ready to practice on the mannequins. For the next hour, both Zac and Dawn take turns attacking each of the many mannequins. Dawn finds sword fighting a lot easier than she expected or could it be that the mannequins are not fighting back. Zac tells her that today's exercise is designed to get her used to the weight of the sword as she swings it around as well as the abruptness of action when the sword hits its mark.

"It is almost noon," Zac says as he reaches for Dawn's sword, "You may want to freshen up in the lavatory."

Dawn looks around the workout room to find a door that looks like it might be a bathroom. She hasn't quite gotten used to the bathroom reference as a 'lavatory' in England.

"Through that opening over there and down a small hallway, the first door on the right is a lavatory," Zac says.

Dawn turns towards the opening as she hears the clanging of the swords being put away. Before entering the opening, she looks back to see Zac making his way across the workout room to the same opening. He, too, needs to freshen up. Dawn enters the first door on the right to find a large lavatory with two sinks and a shower. She looks in the mirror to determine how much 'freshening up' she needs. She doesn't look too bad for all the sword fighting she has done today. She takes her ponytail band out to see if her hair would look better down around her face. Since she didn't curl it, it is a little flat; so it's back into a ponytail. She washes her hands, applies some lotion, and exits the lavatory. Heading back out to the workout room, she feels someone sneaking up behind her. She stops and backs into the hallway wall as Zac pushes himself against her. He kisses her hard as she wraps her arms around his neck. Still in the ecstasy of the moment, Dawn hears a voice through her 'ear bug' which instantly chills the air. By the look on Zac's face, he, too, hears it through his own 'ear bug.'

"Dawn, my dear," she hears, "Are you done with your training?"

It sounds like Aunt Eva. It must be noon.

"Yes," Dawn says as she smiles at Zac, "We'll be right there."

Dawn giggles like a schoolgirl as Zac grabs her hand and pulls her from the opening out into the workout room. Moving quickly across the room, they reach the doors leading to the wide hallway. The banker will undoubtedly be waiting in the library with papers for Dawn to sign.

Sure enough, the library doors are open, and Aunt Eva and a well-dressed man are waiting for her. The man is seated behind a table at the far end of the library. As Dawn approaches with Zac following closely behind, the man stands and extends his hand.

"Hello, Miss Hunter," he says, "I am Charles Entworth. I am your banker. I have some papers that require your signature in order for you to have access to the Fletcher fortune."

He moves from behind the desk and motions for Dawn to move around the table and sit in the chair. After being seated, Mr. Entworth places several papers in front of her in an orderly fashion.

"Please sign here and here and here," he says pointing to signature lines on each paper.

Having done so, Dawn looks up at Mr. Entworth to verify she is done signing. Mr. Entworth gathers the three papers she has just signed, puts them in a large, brown envelope, and places the envelope in his briefcase. He locks the briefcase and looks at Aunt Eva to indicate his business is done.

"Well," Aunt Eva says, "Let's adjourn to the upper patio for lunch."

No sooner has she completed her sentence, than Chumley enters the library to wheel Aunt Eva to the patio. Mr. Entworth follows behind while Dawn walks towards Zac, grabs his hand, and together they bring up the rear. Traveling at their own speeds, the group walks down the wide hallway to the French doors. Another servant opens the doors as the group enters onto the upper patio. The table has already been set, and James and Ms. Johnson are already seated at the table. Chumley wheels Aunt Eva to her place setting while she directs Mr. Entworth to be seated at her left. Dawn and Zac are the last to seat themselves at the table.

After lunch, Mr. Entworth excuses himself as Chumley escorts him out the front door to his automobile. Zac leaves, as well, to fetch his parents from the airport. Ms. Johnson has not quite completed her lunch, so she remains seated; while Dawn, Aunt Eva, and James retreat to the tech lab. This time, they will be going to the lab using Aunt Eva's elevator. This is a new route for Dawn. Just past the French doors in the wide hallway is a long curtain that appears to be covering a large window. James pulls the curtain to expose an elevator door. He pushes a button and the door opens. It is big enough for the three of them to travel upward in comfort. When they reach the second floor, they all exit and move to the other side of another hallway. There is another elevator door that will take them directly to the tech lab.

Once in the lab, James gets the book from the safe while Aunt Eva and Dawn make themselves comfortable around a small table. Remembering the combination, James opens the clasp and sets the book in front of Aunt Eva.

Just as Aunt Eva begins to open the book, Dawn remembers what her mother said to her in her dream.

"I had a dream last night where mother came to me," Dawn tells Aunt Eva, "She told me that she left instructions for me in the last section of the book."

Looking a little surprised, Aunt Eva feathers her fingers down the side of the pages towards the back. She inserts her fingers into the last few pages and opens the book. She looks at the writing and acknowledges that it is Hilda's writing. She turns back a few more pages until she sees writing that no longer looks like Hilda's. She moves the book around so Dawn can read it. Aunt Eva wheels herself from the table and over to the desk where James is running some scans leaving Dawn to interpret the book by herself.

After a couple of hours pass, Aunt Eva sees that Dawn has completed the last section written by her mother. She is now thumbing backwards through the book. Dawn stumbles upon a picture in the book that looks just like her necklace pendant. There is writing underneath the picture that tells of a yellow stone and a blue stone.

"The necklaces," Dawn says as she points to the picture.

Aunt Eva wheels herself excitedly around and back to the table. Dawn turns the book around so Aunt Eva can see the picture of the pendant. Aunt Eva looks at the writing below the picture.

"That's father's writing," Aunt Eva says.

Aunt Eva looks closer at the writing and openly interprets the meaning, "It reads that through the stone is a portal seen, one for day and one for night."

Dawn looks up at Aunt Eva with an 'ah ha' expression on her face. She remembers using the yellow stone to look out her window and finding it had great magnification properties.

"That's it," Dawn says happily, "The stones from our necklaces will show us the way to the portals. My yellow one for day, and your blue one for night."

As Dawn begins to make plans to take her necklace directly out to the hedge to test her theory, Aunt Eva continues reading, "The stone will find the portal but magical energy is needed to enter."

"Magical energy," Dawn says, "So anyone who possesses magical powers probably emits 'magical energy.' That's why Uncle George fell through the hedge. He was probably over the portal. Otherwise, he would have just landed on top."

"Yes," Aunt Eva chimes in, "Even though his powers are not as advanced as yours, his limited powers would still create energy; as would mine and possibly Xavier's. Without the stones in the pendants to show the location of the portal, George cannot get out by himself."

Dawn excitedly looks up at Aunt Eva. Aunt Eva knows exactly what she is thinking.

"That means," Aunt Eva says before Dawn gets the chance, "That Xavier might be able to go through the portal with you. He is not the first born, but he would have magical powers equivalent to mine. Two warriors are always better than one, especially a warrior like him. We had better plan for that possibility. I do believe that he would not want you going in alone. He has become quite fond of you."

"Fond of me," Dawn thinks to herself, "I certainly hope it is more than fondness."

She smiles at Aunt Eva to validate her conclusion that her relationship with Zac is no more than fondness; even though, Dawn is convinced there is love involved. Aunt Eva twirls the book back around in front of her. Dawn thumbs backwards several more pages until she reaches writing that appears to belong to someone else. Aunt Eva verifies that the new writing belongs to her mother. Dawn wants to concentrate on the sections written by her grandmother, her grandfather, and her mother which appear to be more than half the book. So, she goes back to the beginning of her grandmother's section and places a marker. That's where she will begin her magical training.

James takes the book and places it back in the safe. Dawn and Aunt Eva make a plan to test the pendants. They agree to use the pendants to find the portal but not to enter until they are completely ready for the anticipated battle. Knowing that Zac may be able to enter the hedge, he will have to be trained accordingly. They will have to be trained as a team. Dawn smiles at the prospect of being an 'on-the-field' team rather than her on the field and him in the bleachers. This will require, she is hoping, more intimate training time.

Dawn and Aunt Eva decide to test after dinner. Since it will probably be dark, they will use Aunt Eva's pendant; and, of course, they will test Dawn's pendant in the morning. Everything must be understood right down to the tiniest detail. There is no room for error. With magic, they may get only one shot, so to speak.

James announces that it is almost four o'clock. They all will be required to dress formal for dinner. Realizing she only has an hour, Dawn jumps up from the table and motions for James to let her out of the door. She races down the stairs, into the hallways, and to her room. Now knowing the value of her necklace, she decides she must find a safer location for it. The box inside the black bag under her mattress just doesn't seem secure enough. She wonders if there is a safe in her bedroom somewhere. Surely, her mother had jewels that she left here because she certainly didn't have any in the United States. Remembering the 'ear bug' she still had in her ear, she pushes the button on the power unit attached to her sleeve and begins to speak.

"Aunt Eva," she says, "Can you hear me?"

"Yes, my dear," Aunt Eva says into her ear.

"Can anyone else hear me?" she asks wanting to ensure secrecy.

"No," Aunt Eva responds, "You and Xavier are on different frequencies than anyone else, and he has his unit turned off."

"Is there a safe in my bedroom?" Dawn asks, "Knowing the value of my necklace, I need to ensure its security."

"Yes, of course, my dear," Aunt Eva replies, "There is a safe in the closet with your shoes, behind the shoe rack. There is a small lever at the bottom that will slide the shoe rack up and back to expose the safe. The combination, I believe, is etched on the back of the toilet lid under the quilted, satin cover. Your mother had such a sense of humor. She thought no one would sully their hands rummaging around the toilet."

Dawn laughs at the thought. She remembers one time her mother hid the car keys behind the toilet, so she couldn't find them for just that reason. But, Dawn needs to open the safe, so sully her hands, she will! After finding the combination exactly where Aunt Eva said it was, she commits it to memory. After she places the box containing the necklace into the safe and ensures the safe is again camouflaged, she starts to get ready for dinner.

CHAPTER TWENTY

As Dawn stands at the top of the staircase outside her bedroom, she notices that Chumley and Ida are greeting someone at the front door. It is Zac and Lord and Lady Farnsworth. Zac glances up and sees Dawn ready to descend the staircase. His eyes get as big as saucers. He can hardly believe what he is seeing. Dawn is wearing a tight-fitting, blue-sequined gown and a solitary diamond necklace with matching earrings she found in the safe. Her blue, satin heels match the dress perfectly and are clearly visible through a knee-high slit in the front of the dress. Her hair and makeup are flawless. She has become quite proficient in her own beautification. So much so that Zac can't take his eyes off her as she gracefully walks down the stairs. He makes his way to the bottom of the stairs to rapture himself in her presence. When she reaches the proximity of his outstretched hand, Lord and Lady Farnsworth, as well as Ida and Chumley, look up to admire the ravishing view.

"Oh, my," Lord Farnsworth says, "Isn't she a vision."

"Close your mouth, dear," Lady Farnsworth says as she reaches up to lift his chin.

After reaching the bottom, Zac takes her hand and directs her to his father and mother.

"Father, mother," Zac says proudly, "This is Dawn."

Dawn extends her hand in Lord Farnsworth's direction. He grabs her hand and places it under his arm as he walks away to escort her to the dining room. Zac extends his hand to his mother, and they follow Lord Farnsworth and Dawn down the hallway. After placing a hat, a wrap, and coats into the cloak room, Chumley and Ida quickly catch up to follow them along.

As they approach the main dining room, another servant opens both doors to allow entrance inside the room. Knowing that the Farnsworth's have arrived, Aunt Eva has already placed herself at the head of the table. Lord Farnsworth escorts Dawn to the opposite side of the table and insists that she sit next to him. Zac and his mother seat themselves across from them. Moments later, Ms. Johnson and James enter the dining room and make their way to the next seats in order. No sooner have they seated themselves than two servants bring in trays filled with bowls of soup. After the first course has been placed in front of everyone, Lady Farnsworth finds a break in her soup consumption to talk to Dawn.

"We were so sorry to hear about the death of your mother," she says, "We really missed her when she moved to the United States. Your resemblance to her is remarkable. I wanted to imagine she had returned when I saw you walk down those stairs."

"Yes," Lord Farnsworth continues, "She became very good friends with our oldest daughter when we first moved here. She spent a lot of time at our estate. Xavier was almost five years old when your mother left."

"You have an older sister?" Dawn asks as she looks at Zac.

She just now realizes that she doesn't know much about Zac. She has fallen in love with him and plans to go into battle with him but hasn't taken the time to inquire about his life.

Zac nods to acknowledge affirmation that he does indeed have an older sister but doesn't take the time to further converse on the subject. The awkwardness of the immediate silence is broken by the servants who appear to remove the bowls in preparation for placement of the second course. To change the direction of the conversation, Aunt Eva clears her throat to inquire about the Farnsworth's business in London.

"Were you able to meet with Parliament?" Aunt Eva inquires.

Lord Farnsworth replies and they continue talking about all the meetings he attended and what was accomplished. Not being particularly interested in the business conversation, Dawn and Zac begin a conversation of their own. Zac elaborates in more detail about how beautiful Dawn looks, and Dawn timidly accepts his compliments. After two hours of menu course exchanges intermingled with multi-topic pleasantries, Lord and Lady Farnsworth decide it's time to retire to their own estate. When Aunt Eva wheels herself away from the table, Dawn can see she is wearing her blue-stoned pendant. It is a sign that Aunt Eva plans to test the pendant on the hedge, undoubtedly that very evening. While Aunt Eva escorts Lord and Lady Farnsworth from the dining room, Dawn motions for Zac to stay behind. Once everyone has departed the room, Dawn wants to tell Zac about her recent discoveries; so she grabs him and whisks him away to a private corner.

"Yesterday," Dawn whispers, "We unlocked my mother's book of magic; and earlier this afternoon, we were able to interpret the secrets we found there. We are going to test our theory tonight at the hedge. Will you stay and go with us?"

"Most certainly," Zac assures her, "I promised your aunt I would see this through to the end. I'm only sorry I can't do more to help with the battle you are in for."

"That's the best part," Dawn says excitedly and smiles, "In the book, it reads that anyone with magical energy can penetrate the portal. That's how Uncle George ended up in the hedge. He went through the portal. Even though his magical powers are minimal because he is not the first born, they are enough for him to pass through the portal. Aunt Eva said you would have the same amount of magical powers. So, you can go with me. We are a team. We will need to learn to fight as a team. Isn't that great?"

Zac appears to be excited; but more than excitement, he is relieved. During his training session with Dawn, he could only wonder if his training curriculum was going to be adequate. If he can go with her, their chances will double. Maybe triple if any of his magic is useful inside the hedge. Dawn grabs his hand and leads him to the doorway. Just before they reach it, Zac stops and pulls Dawn towards him. He bends down slightly and kisses her. With a visible excitement in his step, he now leads her to the doorway. When in the hallway, they can see that Aunt Eva and the Farnsworth's have reached the front door. Chumley and Ida are helping the Lord and Lady on with their coat and wrap. Zac and Dawn reach the group about the moment Lord Farnsworth puts on his hat.

"I will be staying here for a while," Zac says, "Don't wait up for me."

Lady Farnsworth laughs as if that was ever an option. She knew he would be staying, since he insisted on driving separately.

Chumley opens the front door and watches as Lord and Lady Farnsworth exit the house, walk down the front stairs, and enter their awaiting automobile. When the lights of their automobile disappear in the distance, Chumley shuts the front door. He and Ida excuse themselves as Zac begins to wheel Aunt Eva down the hallway to the back of the house.

"James," Aunt Eva says into her 'ear bug' control bracelet, "Are you ready to go to the hedge?"

"Yes, ma'am," James replies through the speaker in the bracelet, "I'll be right there."

"Meet us at the back patio with the four-seated ATV," Aunt Eva directs.

Aunt Eva motions for Dawn to open the French doors leading to the patio while Zac pushes her through. It is just barely dusk. They look up at the sky to see the outline of the moon that will be more visible when the sun has totally set. Enjoying the cool night air and saying nothing, they wait for James. Moments later they hear the rumbling of the ATV motor. James appears in the ATV at the edge of the patio. Zac wheels Aunt Eva to the edge and helps her into the front seat next to James. He and Dawn get into the back seat.

"Let's start at the west end of the hedge," Aunt Eva says, "Isn't that the general vicinity where George was replacing the sensor when he fell in?"

"Yes," James replies, "I believe it is."

So, off they go with the necklace to the hedge to find the portal. As they approach the west corner of the estate property, Aunt Eva hands her necklace to Dawn. As James drives slowly east, parallel to the hedge, Dawn looks through the blue stone of the pendant into the hedge. She sees nothing but very large, green leaves. She looks up and down the hedge. About one-fourth of the way along the hedge, Dawn begins to see some ripples. She no longer sees leaves, just a large, circular bundle of waves.

"Stop," she says.

James stops the ATV, and she gets out almost catching her heel in the bottom of her dress. She removes her shoes and places them on the back seat floor. Again looking through the stone and finding the ripples, she moves closer to the hedge. She raises her other hand in front of the stone, so she can see if her hand will penetrate the ripples.

"Wait," Zac says, "Let me come with you. I need to know if I will be able to enter the portal."

Zac stands behind Dawn but reaches his arm out to overlap hers. Together they walk closer and closer. Dawn can see the ripples flowing over and around their fingertips. Zac can't see anything, but he can feel the rippling sensation in his fingers. They move closer and closer until both arms are in the ripples to their elbows. At that moment, they both feel a cool breeze rushing passed their hands. Simultaneously, they quickly pull their arms out of the ripples.

"This is it," Dawn excitedly says, "We have found it. We need to mark it."

She looks around for something to use as a marker. The sun has almost entirely set so it is difficult to see anything in the dark. James turns the ATV around and uses the headlights to illuminate the area for a marker. Zac sees a large rock at the corner of a walkway in the rose garden about a hundred feet away. Zac jumps into the ATV and directs James to take him to the rock which he loads into the back seat. Dawn stays at the hedge as a temporary marker until the ATV returns. Zac places the rock where Dawn is standing.

"Let's come back tomorrow to test the other pendant," Aunt Eva suggests, "We need to know they both work the same way. Since we are not sure of the timing inside the hedge, we may need to use either or both necklaces. According to the writing in the book, we concluded the yellow stone is for day and the blue stone is for night."

With that, Dawn and Zac get back into the ATV. It is apparent by the look on his face that he is elated that his portal experience has assured him he will be able to accompany Dawn through the hedge. Instead of going all the way around the rose garden and the bushes and trees, James decides to turn around and return to the patio the same way he came. He stops the ATV at the edge of the patio as Dawn grabs her shoes and Zac helps Aunt Eva into her wheelchair. As Zac wheels Aunt Eva across the patio with Dawn following barefoot, they can hear the ATV motor dwindle into silence in the distant darkness. Ida is waiting inside the French doors to escort Aunt Eva to her room. As Ida turns Aunt Eva's wheelchair down another hallway, Dawn and Zac continue on towards the front door. Chumley is waiting there with Zac's overcoat.

"You may retire, Chumley," Dawn says, "I will make sure the front door is locked."

She knows the door locks are automatic, but she was trying to gracefully excuse Chumley from his duties. Zac takes his coat from Chumley and waits until he disappears down the hallway. Dawn puts on her shoes and escorts Zac out the front door to the porch. The driveway is so well lit that it almost looks like daytime. Dawn can see Zac's Mercedes convertible off to the right. Zac turns towards Dawn and grabs her by both hands.

"This is just brilliant," Zac says, "I didn't expect that your presence here was going to be so overwhelming. Our families have waited almost twenty-five years for this curse to end. I know your grandparents and your mother would be so proud of you; and even though it has been a short time, I have fallen in love with you."

As her eyes fill with tears, she says, "I love you, too."

Zac kisses her softly and walks down the front stairs. Dawn watches as he gets into his Mercedes and starts the motor. She stays on the porch until she can no longer see his lights in the distance. She goes back inside the house, shuts the front door, and heads up the stairs to her bedroom. Halfway up the stairs, she can hear the loud clicking of the front door locks as they automatically activate.

CHAPTER TWENTY-ONE

Dawn and Aunt Eva have tested the yellow stone for access into the portal. It works the same as the blue stone. They are confident that access through the portal is assured. Dawn is ever more aware that the contents of the book are going to be critical to her mission. She will study it intently. She has decided she will spend the next few weeks doing physical training with Zac in the mornings and concentrate deeply on her mental training in the afternoons. In the meantime, James and Aunt Eva will monitor the hedge for changes in activity. Time is limited, and they are assured they may get only one chance to end this prophecy. If they don't succeed, both families are doomed.

As planned, Dawn is diligent in her physical training with Zac. She has become very proficient using the sword but excels in the use of the bow and arrows. The gun is a little heavy and too noisy for Dawn, but she can hit her mark in a pinch. She knows that the use of weapons is a precursor to using magic. The use of magic systematically depletes the body of energy. The plan is to eliminate as many enemy soldiers using weapons so as to save her magical energy to battle the witch. Dawn doesn't realize the extent of her magical capabilities but will try to test them before entering the hedge.

Dawn has learned through the writings in the book that there are specific words and chants called 'magicology' required to activate her internal powers. With various arm movements and sudden extensions of her hands, magical powers will flow out to penetrate the persons or objects of the intended spell. To test this, out of the purview of anyone on the estate, Dawn has decided to use the roof as her testing arena.

Dawn has read, word for word, all the writings of her grandmother, her grandfather, and her mother making notes of words and chants she knows she will need. She decides to read the writings in the first part of the book; the ones written by many past generations of the Fletcher family. Some of them are ancient and reflect spells that are more conducive to the ways of olden times. She finds recipes for potions to heal many plagues and illnesses from earlier centuries. None of which will be necessary in her day and age, but she reads about them anyway. Dawn takes the notes she has written and decides to devote the next week using them to hone her magical powers. She folds the notes and places them into her pants' pocket.

Before she leaves the tech lab, she decides to see what progress James has made analyzing the activity in the hedge. She stands behind James and looks up at the monitor on the wall. James has placed a 'red spot' on the diagram of the hedge where he believes the portal is. It is on the left side of the grid. On the right side of the grid, the splotches are bundled in some places and spread out in other places; but they take up the biggest part of the right side. Switching from screen to screen of different, grid timeframes, James shows Dawn how the activity of the splotches changes during different periods of time.

"What does that mean?" Dawn inquires.

"Well," James replies, "There are specific areas on the grid where the splotches are consistent. They never seem to go past a

certain part of the grid. I'm not sure if
there is a barrier inside the hedge or what.
You need to be aware of it, so you can prepare
for it. Hopefully, your 'ear bug' will work
inside the hedge. If it does, I can make you
aware of the barrier before you get to it. If
not, at least you know about it."

"Have you seen any more evidence of Uncle
George's 'ear bug'?" Dawn asks.

"No," James answers, "I suspect the
battery in the 'ear bug' has died by now. I
have put a yellow marker at the places I saw
the blinking light. As you can see on the
grid, they are in the far left section of the
grid. I would expect to see some body heat
splotches in this area if George was there and
alive. Unless he has been captured by the
witch's army and is one of those splotches on
the right side, he may be dead or hiding. We
will analyze the grid a little more in depth
tomorrow. I have written a program that will
compare the size of the splotches against the
overall size of the grid to get an idea of how
much territory you will be covering inside the
hedge."

With that, Dawn decides to adjourn to the
roof to test some of the spells and chants she
has committed to memory. She makes her way
through hallways and up staircases until she
reaches the one door that leads to the roof.
She opens the door and walks out to the large,
veranda-type rooftop. She looks around
intently observing things she missed when Zac
took her to the roof. There is an old, cast-
iron table and matching chairs stacked upon
each other in the far corner of the area.
There are some birds nesting in the eaves and
some empty flower pots. There isn't much to
work with, but this should get Dawn started.

She stands in the middle and decides to start with something small. There are some leaves and twigs towards the brick wall at the edge of the roof. She wants to move them to the right just a short distance.

"Purolarano," Dawn says as she swishes her arms slowly to the right.

The leaves and twigs begin to slowly move across the roof but end when Dawn's arm movement stops. Dawn can feel the small thrust of energy emit from her hands. When she stops, the energy stops. Now she knows how it works, so she will have to practice the control. She decides to try something heavier. Maybe a cast-iron chair. Calculating in her mind that her thrust should be more intense, she repeats the magicology while swirling both arms wildly from one side, in the direction of the chairs, to the other. Before she stops the inertial motion of her arms, she can see that the entire table and stacked chairs are rapidly moving across the floor. She quickly stops her arms to avoid sending the table and chairs over the edge of the roof. She now knows the difference in the energy flow for moving small items slowly and large items rapidly.

For about an hour, she tries moving anything she can find on the roof. She feels confident she can now gauge the level of energy she needs to project objects according to their weight and the distance she wants to move them. Seeing that the sun is going down in the distance, Dawn decides she has practiced enough for today. She exits through the door and makes her way down to the main floor hallway. She feels very fatigued from all the exertion; but more than that, she is a little hungry. She decides to get a snack from the kitchen. As she turns into the hallway leading to the kitchen, she bumps into Ms. Johnson.

"Oh, Nancy," Dawn says politely, "I haven't seen you for a while. I suppose the business of the estate is keeping you very busy. I do appreciate your help in looking after things. I am going to the kitchen for a snack. Would you like to join me?"

"Yes," Ms. Johnson replies, "That would be lovely."

Dawn turns and heads towards the kitchen as Ms. Johnson follows behind. Once in the kitchen, Dawn looks around for the refrigerator. The kitchen is so large that Dawn has to look around a couple of corners to find it. Ms. Johnson finds a seat at a small table in the middle of the kitchen. Dawn rummages through the refrigerator to find sandwich makings. She finds bread, meat, cheese, lettuce, tomatoes, and mayonnaise. With her arms full of stuff, she makes her way to a counter next to the table. She spreads everything out and begins to make sandwiches. While she is making the final cuts to the sandwiches and placing them on a plate, Ms. Johnson is opening cupboards to find some chips. Dawn sets both sandwich plates on the table, one for her and one for Ms. Johnson. Ms. Johnson places the chips in a large bowl, and Dawn gets two glasses for some milk.

When both are satisfied they have all they need, they sit down at the table and begin eating. With a break in the food consumption, Ms. Johnson takes the opportunity to catch up on Dawn's progress. Since they arrived at the estate, Ms. Johnson has had very little contact with Dawn. Aunt Eva has had her doing other things in other directions.

"Has the book been beneficial to you?" Ms. Johnson inquires.

Not wanting to provide any in-depth information about the book, Dawn wants to satisfactorily answer the question so that Ms. Johnson will require no further consideration on the subject.

"The book is very interesting and personal," Dawn explains, "It is a journal of sorts. Writings from my mother. Things she wants me to remember and examples to live by."

Ms. Johnson isn't entirely sure that's everything in the book, but she finds she has no follow-up question to extract more information. So, she continues eating her sandwich and watches Dawn as she does the same.

Ms. Johnson finishes her snack first. She puts her plate and glass in the sink and returns to the table. She waits as Dawn puts the last bite of sandwich in her mouth. She gets Dawn's plate and glass and takes them to the sink. While Dawn wipes her hands and mouth on a paper towel, she walks towards the kitchen exit. Ms. Johnson follows. After they both enter the wide hallway, Ms. Johnson thanks Dawn for the snack and heads down one hallway while Dawn continues walking in the wide hallway towards the front foyer and her staircase. As she walks up the staircase, she can hear the paper with her magical notes rustle in her pants' pocket. She needs to remember to put them in a safe place. Dawn enters the bedroom and prepares for bed. Rather than open the safe to put her notes in, she decides to put them under her pillow. They should be safe there.

CHAPTER TWENTY-TWO

Another day is at hand, and Dawn is ready for it. She makes her way to the small dining room for breakfast. As usual, she expects to meet Zac there for their daily training session. It has been almost four weeks since she left home. Time seems to be flying by, but she has certainly accomplished a lot in that short time. According to the prophecy, she only has a few more months to complete her mission. She feels she is almost ready. Her weaponry skills are astounding even though she has no previous experience with any weapons. Dawn is assured that is because of Zac's magnificent, training prowess. It doesn't hurt that her feelings for him provide an extra incentive to excel in her endeavor. Besides, it has been as much fun as it has work. She could spend all day, every day with him with no effort.

As Dawn enters the dining room, she sees that everyone, except Ms. Johnson, is there. She is not always there before Aunt Eva or James, but she is always there before Zac. Her timing must be off. They all look up to see Dawn enter the dining room. It appears they have been discussing something.

"What did I miss?" Dawn says as she seats herself.

"Xavier came over early this morning," Aunt Eva explains, "To report a sighting on the river."

"Yes," Zac continues, "Some people in a boat stopped in my backyard last night. I was out in the boat house watching the river. They said they could see lightning sparks coming from the back side of your hedge as they passed. They were wondering if there was a party at the Fletcher estate. I told them there was no party, but that the gardener sometimes sets off fireworks to scare varmints. I didn't want them to get suspicious and try to wander into your property."

"Good thinking," Aunt Eva commends, "We don't need people nosing around here, especially now. Zac tells me that your weapons training is almost complete, my dear. You have learned a great deal in a short period of time. I should have known. Your mother was a very quick learner. It must come with being the first born. Anyway, we may be able to start your journey sooner than we expected. That will give us a cushion if something goes wrong. James will check the computerized grid of the hedge to see if there was any electric energy surfacing last night."

James nods and begins eating his breakfast as Ms. Johnson enters the room. The immediate silence as she enters makes her suspicious of their topic of discussion before she entered. Dawn can see the confused look on her face. She is always careful what she says to Ms. Johnson, but she would like to know how involved she really is in this project. She makes a mental note to discuss it with Aunt Eva when they go to the lab later this afternoon. Dawn looks over at Zac who has completed his breakfast. He looks over at her and sees that she is fiddling with her eggs. He gets up from the table to give Dawn the signal that if she is ready for their morning workout, so is he. Dawn wipes her mouth with a napkin and walks away from the table to meet Zac at the door. They both excuse themselves and quickly exit the room.

While in the hallway as they make their way to the workout room, Zac takes Dawn's hand and gives it a tender kiss.

"Are you alright?" Zac asks, "You seem a little distant this morning. Are you nervous about the closeness of our journey?"

"Not really nervous about the closeness," Dawn says, "Just apprehensive about the unknown. We are getting closer, and I want to make sure I am one-hundred percent ready. A lot depends on us. I have never had this kind of responsibility before. I know I cannot do it without you."

As they enter the workout room, Zac lets go of Dawn's hand and bends down to kiss her hoping that it will reassure her that he will be at her side always. Dawn smiles and immediately feels better.

"Let's work on rope climbing today," Dawn suggests, "I have a notion there may be some climbing to do inside the hedge."

Dawn tells Zac about the barrier that James found in his computerized grid. It could be a wall they will need to climb or a cliff they will need to descend. Either way, it wouldn't hurt to develop their climbing technique. They walk to the far corner of the room where several, knotted ropes are hanging from the rafters. They each take a rope and begin climbing. Zac, with his voluminous muscles, has no problem ascending the rope. Dawn, however, seems to have trouble grasping the thick rope in her tiny hands. Through the struggle of trying to pull herself up the rope, Dawn remembers a magicology that was used many years ago to help a person ascend castle walls. She decides to try it.

"Econglumello," Dawn whispers to herself.

Just then, Dawn can feel faint, energy waves extend from her hands into the rope as an adhesive. As she pulls each hand away from the rope and extends it up farther, she is using very little of her own physical energy to ascend the rope. Within moments, she has reached the top of the rope. As Zac reaches the top of his rope, he looks over to see that Dawn is waiting with a smile.

"What took ya?" she says."

"How did you do that?" Zac asks in disbelief.

"It's magic," she says with a laugh.

They both laugh out loud and begin to descend the rope. Once again, Dawn beats Zac down the rope using her magic. She now realizes that some of that old magic may come in handy. She decides to conscientiously reflect on the older section of the book. After ascending and descending the rope several more times, Dawn and Zac decide to take a break. They walk to the opposite corner of the room where there is a cooler filled with water, juice, cola, and other beverages. Dawn takes a diet cola while Zac takes a bottle of water. They walk outside to the patio and seat themselves on chaise lounge chairs.

"Tell me about your sister," Dawn says.

"Well," Zac begins, "She is much older than I. Her name is Celeste. Because I was only four and a half at the time, Aunt Eva has filled me in on many things over the years. My sister was the first born, so she inherited the magic just like your mother. Your mother befriended my sister when our family moved into the next estate. When you told me about your grandfather trying to eliminate magic from his life, I was already aware. My father and mother joined in his endeavor. They all knew the damage that could be done with magic. I also knew about your grandmother and mother practicing magic in the basement of this very estate, because my sister would come over and practice with them unbeknownst to my father and mother. As Aunt Eva tells it, after your mother moved to the United States, my sister disappeared. At first, they thought she may have gone with your mother. But communications with your mother confirmed she did not. We don't know where she is or what happened to her."

"Wow," Dawn says, "How mysterious."

"Yes," Zac replies, "But we need to focus on the endeavor at hand."

With that, Zac arises from his chair. He reaches his arm out to help Dawn out of hers. He pulls her close and kisses her. As they stand on the patio taking advantage of this romantic moment, she can hear Aunt Eva in her 'ear bug.' As she looks at Zac, it is apparent he can hear her, too. It never fails; their romantic interludes seem to always be interrupted. Could it be just bad luck? Well, whatever, romance will undoubtedly have to wait. It is true; they need to keep their minds on the trophy.

"We have some important information," Aunt Eva says through the 'ear bugs.' Both you and Zac come to the tech lab. We will be having lunch here."

Both Dawn and Zac walk back across the patio and into the workout room. They cross the workout room and exit into the hallway. Laughing and joking all the way, they find themselves in front of the windowed door. Dawn pushes the buzzer and waits until James comes to open the door. Once inside, Dawn can see that lunch has been placed on one of the tables in the far corner. Zac quickly makes his way past James and Dawn to admire the lunch table.

"I am starving," Zac says as he looks over the food arrangements on the table.

Before Dawn has even made her way to the table, Zac is piling sandwiches and salads on a plate. She giggles as she begins to fill a plate of her own. With plates in hand, Dawn and Zac walk over to the desk in front of the monitor. They can see a cursor running back and forth on the screen. It started at the top and has made its way down the screen about halfway.

"This is the final scan using the program I created to determine the land distance inside the hedge," James says, "It occurred to me one day that the size of the splotches are so small that there has to be a greater land mass inside than just what we see from the outside."

"So you're saying," Zac says between bites of sandwich, "that we may have to travel a great distance when we are on the inside."

"Yes, that's right," James replies, "If we can determine exactly what distances to expect, we can better prepare you for the journey."

Just then, a melodic ding came from the computer indicating the completion of the scan. James clicks the mouse to reveal a menu. He directs the computer to print a final report. When the printer spits out the requested information, James is there to retrieve the report.

"Oh, bloody hey," James says, "That is a little more area than I had expected."

"How big?" Zac inquires.

"Three point two kilometers by eleven point three kilometers," James replies.

"What's that in English?" Dawn interjects.

"That's about two miles wide by seven miles long," James says, "That means the portal is about one mile from the left side of the grid. So, there is about six miles of area you will need to travel to get to the other side. However, that barrier we discussed the other day is about two and a half miles past the portal entrance. Once you get past the barrier, you will undoubtedly encounter the splotches."

"Splotches?" Zac says with a mouthful of salad.

"We're assuming these splotches are the witch's army she has accumulated over the years," James responds, "Possibly changing squirrels and such into fighting soldiers."

"I didn't think there would be so many of them," Zac says after swallowing his salad.

While James and Zac are working out the dynamics of the battlefield, Dawn and Aunt Eva are lunching at an adjoining table. After completing the last bit of potato salad on her plate, Dawn sets her plate aside and leans across the table to confide in Aunt Eva.

"I need to know how much magic I can depend on from Zac," Dawn begins, "I'm guessing he would have the same as you have. How much did your mother teach you when you would go to the basement? What kind of things could you do using your magic?"

"Well," Aunt Eva replies, "Like I said, I didn't have near the powers that your mother had; but, I seemed to be more powerful when your mother was with me. One time when Hilda had gone over to the Farnsworth's, my mother and I went to the basement to practice some magic. I was able to move small objects towards me and away from me. I would transport small pots from the shelf into the air, retrieve them, and return them back to the shelf. That was about the extent of my powers."

"I don't think Zac has had any training or subjected to any magic," Dawn says, "What kind of training can I give him to expose his magical skills?"

"Maybe start out with the same training you started with," Aunt Eva replies, "Take him to the roof and have him try to move things, as you did."

"How did you know I was practicing on the roof?" Dawn says surprisingly.

"One of these days, you are going to know the whereabouts of all the security cameras," Aunt Eva admits, "They are pretty much everywhere, and someone is monitoring them all the time."

Dawn can see that Zac and James have completed their analysis of the grid and recent scan results. She walks over to the desk where Zac is standing behind James. She grabs Zac's hand and stands next to him to eavesdrop on any final discoveries or plans of action.

"Did you find any evidence of electrical activity that would explain the lightning sparks seen last night coming from the hedge?" Dawn asks.

"There was a blip in my status recordings about eight thirty last night," James responds, "Until Zac mentioned someone seeing lightning sparks coming from the hedge, I just thought the blip was a computer error. When I looked closer at the blip, I could see a short burst of electrical energy."

"What could it be?" Zac asks.

"Well, it could be a number of things," James answers, "It could be the witch using magic to build a bigger army, or maybe she is trying to penetrate the outside barrier of the hedge. I haven't seen any weakening of the barrier structure, so I'm sure her attempts are unsuccessful."

James minimizes the grid from the large monitor and walks over to the lunch table to fill a plate. He has been conferring with Zac for so long he hasn't had a chance to get lunch. Once he gets a plateful of luncheon delicacies, he sits at the table with Aunt Eva. Not wanting to disturb James to let them out of the door, Dawn signals to him and Aunt Eva that she and Zac will take the elevator. Once in the elevator, Dawn tells Zac of her plan to test his magical powers.

"Instead of our regular workout session in the morning," Dawn begins, "We need to see what magical powers you have, so I thought we could work on the roof."

"Oh, the dark, secluded roof, ay?" Zac says with a devilish smile, "Are you sure it's my magical powers you want to see?"

As the elevator door opens, Dawns exits first with her hands covering her cheeks. She is blushing with embarrassment. Zac follows and grabs her arm. He pulls her around to see that she is smiling but still embarrassed.

"One day," she says, "You, as well as I, will know the existence of every security camera in this place. But for now, please know there is one on the roof; and I've been told, someone is always watching."

Dawn can see the excitement drain quickly from Zac's face. It is obvious she has really burst his balloon. By the time they reach the front door, they both are back to normal. Zac kisses Dawn goodbye and winks as he exits. Dawn waves as the door closes tightly, and she makes her way up the staircase to her room.

CHAPTER TWENTY-THREE

The next morning is like any other except Dawn will be the teacher today. She goes to the small dining room for breakfast where she will meet up with Zac. Before she went to sleep the night before, she wrote down some magicology she thought Zac would be capable of associating to his magical powers. As she enters the dining room, she sees that only Aunt Eva and James are there.

"Where is Nancy?" Dawn asks as she seats herself at the table.

"I have sent her to London on business," Aunt Eva replies.

"Maybe this is a good opportunity to ask about her," Dawn says, "I find her to be somewhat mysterious. At times I think she is friendly and caring, and then other times I find her to be withdrawn and unhappy. I never know how to approach her."

"Nancy came to work for my father just after your mother left for the United States," Aunt Eva begins, "I'm not really sure where she came from. I know her parents are dead, and she graduated from Oxford University. My father trusted her, and she has been very loyal as far as I can tell. I was living with my husband at the estate west of here, so I didn't get involved with things at the main estate. She seemed to take care of things adequately and still does today. We have limited the knowledge of our family secrets to you, me, James, and Zac; and, of course, Zac's mother and father. So, I think Nancy may feel paranoid when we all seem to go about our business in secrecy. She has, upon occasion, made inquiries about what we are doing and appears unsatisfied with our general responses."

"What does she know about the book?" Dawn asks, "From the first day she asked me to find the book, she has been particularly interested in its contents. I even had a dream that she took the book from me and tried to open it."

"I told her the book was taken to the United States by your mother and contained some old, family genealogical and financial history that my father wanted to keep safe," Aunt Eva replies, "But I'm not sure she believed that. In any event, I don't trust anyone outside the four of us."

At that moment, Zac enters the dining room with his usual smiling face and lilting step. He seats himself next to Dawn and awaits arrival of his breakfast. He can see that Dawn has not yet been served, so he assumes she must have only recently arrived in the room herself. No sooner does he sit down, than two plates are placed in front of them both. It is Eggs Benedict and fruit today; Zac's favorite.

"You two will continue your training, today," Aunt Eva says, "James and I will be in the tech lab constructing a virtual map, of sorts, of the inside of the hedge. It may not be exact, but it may give a general idea of distances and terrain you may encounter. So, let's meet in the lab again at lunchtime."

Having completed their breakfasts, James and Aunt Eva leave the dining room. Zac has made a big dent in his breakfast plate while Dawn's consumption is barely noticeable. Zac stops eating for a moment to look over at Dawn. She is placing a strawberry in her mouth as she turns to see Zac staring at her.

"So, I guess it is the roof for us this morning, ay?" Zac inquires.

After swallowing the piece of strawberry, Dawn replies, "Yes, it is. How is the weather outside today?"

"Just beautiful," Zac says as he leans over to stare more closely at Dawn, "And the weather's great, too."

Dawn nudges Zac with her elbow to indicate her embarrassment at the compliment he so graciously extends. Dawn finds a new attribute in Zac almost every day. He is handsome, intelligent, gracious, considerate, well-built, patient, thoughtful, and she could go on and on. She decides he is just perfect, and she is so grateful he is interested in her. Zac finishes his breakfast and waits quietly while Dawn completes her plate of fruit and drinks her juice. As they get up to leave the room, a servant comes in to clear the table of dishes. Dawn and Zac pass the servant and exit the dining room. Outside in the hallway, they route themselves to the roof.

As Zac closes the door to the roof, Dawn extracts a piece of paper from her pocket. She opens it and hands it to Zac. Zac takes one look at it and ganders back at Dawn in puzzlement.

"What is this?" he asks.

"That is magicology," Dawn replies.

"Magicwhatogy?" Zac asks with a laugh.

"It's magicology," Dawn again replies, "It's terminology used in the performance of magic. I got them from the book. Depending upon your level of magical powers, some of them may not work for you."

"Pur – o – lar – an – o," Zac slowly enunciates the first word on the paper.

"Purolarano," Dawn repeats, "Saying that, along with various hand and arm movements, should allow you to move objects around; either towards you or away from you. So, let's try it. Watch me."

Dawn points to a small flower pot in the window sill. She extends her arm towards the pot.

"Purolarano," she says as she slowly moves her hand towards the middle of the roof floor.

The pot levitates from the sill and moves slowly in the direction of Dawn's arm movement. She lowers her hand to place the pot gently on the floor. To give Zac a sense of contrast in the intensity of arm movements, Dawn gives the command again but is more extreme with her motions. She lifts the pot from the floor; and with quicker, more definite, movement, she hurls the pot across the roof into the adjacent wall. The pot crashes into the wall and falls in pieces onto the floor.

"Bloody hey," Zac says obviously impressed, "Can I do that?"

"Well," Dawn says, "We'll see. Now you try it. After you have said the word and have extended your arm or arms towards the object, you will feel a tingling of energy shoot from the tips of your fingers. Once you experience that feeling, you can adjust intensity of movement to compensate for size and weight of objects you wish to move."

Zac looks around the roof for something small to start with. He sees a wire plant holder in the corner. He extends one arm out towards the holder.

"Purolarano," he says.

Just as Dawn had said, he can feel the
tingling in his fingertips. He doesn't dare
move his arm yet. He wants to relish in the
feeling so he can gauge the difference in the
intensity of every motion. He begins to
slowly move his arm away from the corner where
the holder is situated. The holder begins to
slowly move at the same speed as Zac's arm.
He moves the holder about two feet, then
stops. He looks over at Dawn and smiles. He
is particularly pleased with himself. Still
holding his arm out, he starts the motion
again. This time he moves his arm a little
faster. Again, the holder moves at the faster
speed. Feeling very brave, he thrusts his arm
across his body very fast. He quickly stops
his arm movement only to watch the plant
holder flip over the edge of the roof.

"Oops," Zac says as he and Dawn run to
the brick wall at the edge of the roof and
look over.

They can see the plant holder broken in
pieces on the patio below. There is no one
around to witness the folly of Zac's magical
training. Dawn and Zac laugh at his attempt
to progress his training a little more quickly
just as she had done. Dawn assures him that
with practice he will feel the different
levels of energy and be able to control the
movement. So, together they spend the next
two hours moving objects back and forth across
the rooftop. Zac is becoming very proficient
in his control and is taking his training very
seriously. He knows how important even his
small amount of magical abilities may be
during their quest.

It is eleven thirty, and Dawn wants to
give Zac an opportunity to use the magicology
that will allow him to adhere to a surface;

like the one she uses climbing the rope. If
his magical powers extend to this level, he
will be able to propel himself over walls or
down ravines. The more self-reliant he can
be, the easier it is going to be on Dawn.
This may be the cushion he was talking about.
If Dawn's powers are as great as the witches,
then Zac's powers will give them that little
extra. When Zac tries to use his powers to
climb the ropes and walls in the workout room,
Dawn can see his magical energy is
diminishing. His limited powers will not
allow the same stamina afforded to Dawn. To
put Zac out of his misery or save him from
embarrassment, Dawn ends their training
session by assuring him they are needed in the
tech lab.

Once inside the lab, Zac makes his way
directly to the food table, as usual. Dawn
meanders to a table where Aunt Eva and James
are looking at a large chart. The chart
covers almost the entire table. James looks
at Dawn when she reaches the table. He pulls
a retractable pointer from his pocket.

"This is the virtual map of inside the
hedge that your aunt was talking about," James
says as he extends the pointer, "Using the
area distance calculations and other various
information recorded over the past several
months, I have been able to put together a map
to show what I suspect to be hills and dales
and possible structures."

As he is talking, he points to sections
of the map and describes them as highlands,
then moves on to indicate lowlands, and
circles with the pointer to reflect structures
of some sort.

"I will be miniaturizing this map," James
says, "So you can take it with you. It would

be more effective if you could commit to memory as much of this map as possible. You may not have many opportunities to stop and read it."

Just then, Zac walks up to the table and stands next to Dawn. He has a plateful of food which is double his usual amount. He places the plate in front of Dawn to indicate he has fetched lunch for both of them. She takes one of the chicken salad croissants and begins eating as she watches James continue his narrative of the map. Zac holds the plate and eats the other croissant as he, too, watches James.

After James has fully briefed everyone about the map, he and Aunt Eva make their way to the food table to gather their own lunches. Meanwhile, Dawn and Zac are going over and over the map to coordinate their understanding of the possible terrain awaiting them. When they have ingested as much information from the map that they can, Dawn walks over to the table where Aunt Eva and James are seated eating their lunches. She reports to them the progress Zac has made with his magic. Just as she is about to tell them of the plant holder that is now spread all over the lower patio, Zac quickly steps behind her and covers her mouth.

"Well," he says, "We must go. More magic to practice. Now that we have a general idea of what to expect inside the hedge, we can apply our magic and weaponry more effectively."

Zac grabs Dawn by the hand and hurriedly escorts her to the elevator. He doesn't want James to have to leave his lunch to open the back doors. Aunt Eva waves with a puzzled look as James continues eating his lunch.

Once inside the elevator, Zac pulls Dawn close to him and kisses her. He doesn't stop kissing her until the elevator doors open when they reach the second floor. They exit this elevator and take the next elevator to the main floor. As they step out, Zac again grabs Dawn's hand and quickly walks towards the hallway leading to the workout room.

"Let's go practice some magic and weaponry," Zac says, "I am feeling very confident that there will be no more broken plant holders."

With that, they enter the workout room and spend the rest of the day practicing.

CHAPTER TWENTY-FOUR

It's morning again; and Dawn takes note,
as she arises this day, of the amount of time
that has passed since she arrived at the
estate. It has been almost three months.
Just short of actually destroying anyone, like
she will have to do to the witch inside the
hedge, she is very confident that she has
developed the full extent of her magical
skills. She has been able to do some
miraculous things. She is totally aware of
the limits of Zac's powers. Her use of
weapons has also reached a plateau. She feels
secure that there is not much more they can
prepare for on this side of the hedge. She
knows there will be unknowns inside the hedge
but hopes they have considered almost
everything. But, knowing she can't predict
the future, she consuls herself in the
knowledge that she has made every effort to
account for any possible occurrence.

Dawn gets ready for the day as usual and
makes her way to the small dining room. Aunt
Eva has sent Ms. Johnson to London again on
business. This is a clue that Aunt Eva has
secret family matters to discuss. Dawn seats
herself at the table to immediately receive
her plate of breakfast. She knows that
nothing will be discussed until Zac has
arrived. Aunt Eva doesn't like repeating
herself. Just as Dawn reaches for her orange
juice, Zac enters the dining room. He sits
next to Dawn, as usual, and awaits his
breakfast. After Zac has received his plate
and begins to cut his breakfast steak, Aunt
Eva clears her throat to begin her daily
outline of instructions.

"I think we are ready," she begins, "James and I have made a checklist of all points of consideration. We have accomplished everything on the list, so we should spend today planning the 'zero hour.' How do you both feel? Do you think you are ready?"

Aunt Eva and James look directly at Dawn and Zac to see if they detect any apprehension in their body language. Dawn and Zac look at each other in a moment of seriousness that the day has come to put all their training to the purpose intended. Are they, indeed, ready?

"Yes," Dawn says most confidently, "We are ready."

"Well, then," Aunt Eva responds, "We will meet in the lab after breakfast. Using some tricks I found in the book, I have designed some combat gear for you to wear. It should provide protection for suspected elements inside the hedge as well as flexibility to maneuver most comfortably."

"Combat gear?" Dawn inquires, "You really have thought of everything. I feel most assured that we are as prepared as we will ever be."

"I know this is a great burden on you, my dear," Aunt Eva says to Dawn, "But I see so much of your mother in you. She had every intention of returning to England to fulfill the family prophecy, I am sure. But, at a time when she knew she would not return, she had all the confidence that you would be able to take her place."

"I know," Dawn says, "This whole adventure has made a new person of me. I know it is a lot to take in, but I feel such an attachment that I have never had before. When I think back, I realize that my mother was trying to prepare me for something. I know she will be with me in heart and mind."

They all sit quietly and finish their breakfasts. After which, they adjourn to the lab. As they exit the elevator, Dawn can see two mannequins across the room. On them are outfits made of black leather with straps, belts, rivets, and zippers. On the table next to the mannequins, there are arrow quivers, gun holsters, and sword sheaths also made of black leather. As Dawn and Zac make their way to get a closer look at the outfits, Aunt Eva and James plant themselves at the desk in front of the large monitor. James brings up a diagram of the outfits. Dawn touches the outfit she knows must be hers.

"Wow," she says, "What is this fabric? It looks like leather but it feels so soft; not stiff."

"Some time ago," Aunt Eva explains, "I found instructions in the book to produce some fabric that was light and soft but had the strength of a 'Kevlar' vest. Using some ingredients my magic was able to produce, I collaborated with my miller to make the fabric you see there. Try them on."

Dawn and Zac take their respective outfits from the mannequins into separate adjoining rooms. When they reappear wearing the outfits, Aunt Eva and James are obviously pleased with the fit.

"This diagram shows the placement of your weapons and other incidentals you may need," James explains.

Both Dawn and Zac walk to the desk to study the diagram. After they are sure they have sufficiently memorized the locations of belts and straps, they both go to the table where the weapon holders are and begin belting, strapping, and zipping them to their outfits. Everything is located in very strategic places making the outfit as compact and comfortable as possible given all the stuff that will be attached to it.

"These are great," Dawn says, "I feel like conquering the world."

"Not the world, my dear," Aunt Eva replies, "Just a very wicked witch."

Dawn continues to examine the outfit for pockets and pouches and plans in her mind which things will go where. Zac does the same. They both return to the dressing rooms and remove their combat gear. They place them back on the mannequins and the weapon holders on the table. While Zac is finishing his gear return, Dawn walks to the desk and sits in a chair next to Aunt Eva.

"Are there any remnants of magic left in the basement where grandmother would practice?" Dawn asks Aunt Eva.

"I haven't been down there for years," Aunt Eva replies, "But I would imagine there is something still there. It has been securely locked, so no one could have disturbed anything."

"I would like to take a look," Dawn says, "I remember some recipes from the book that I would like to try. If they work, they might be helpful concoctions to take with us."

"The key to the basement is in the safe with the book," Aunt Eva reports, "James will get the key for you."

With that, James walks to the safe, opens it, and retrieves a key. He returns to the desk handing the key to Dawn. Dawn motions for Zac to follow, and they both exit via the elevator.

"Do you know where the door to the basement is?" Dawn asks Zac as they exit into the main hallway.

"Well," Zac replies, "There is only one place it is likely to be."

Zac walks in the direction of the kitchen as Dawn follows close behind. Luckily, there is no one in the kitchen to inquire about their secret mission. Zac continues through the kitchen to a door leading into a very large pantry. At the far end of the pantry in a corner is a wooden door with an old padlock. There is a large, potato bin in front of it that Zac has to move before they can unlock and enter the door. The bin is a little heavier than Zac can move by himself, so Dawn takes one side to provide added strength. Together, they are able to move the bin. Dawn takes the key from her pocket and places it in the padlock. Sure enough, the key opens the lock. Zac opens the door and walks in ahead of Dawn. It is very dark, so Zac reaches around to find a light switch of some kind. As he progresses into the room, he feels a string with a metal cap at the end touch his forehead. He pulls the string which illuminates a bulb just above their heads. This provides enough light to see a downward staircase just ahead. They can see a row of light switches on the wall at the top of the staircase. Zac walks towards the switches and begins to flip them. With each flip, lights down the stairs and on into the basement area provide enough brightness to see the entire area. Zac proceeds to descend the old, wooden stairs. They creak with every step. Dawn follows closely behind. They both stop at the bottom and look intently around the room.

There are old, wooden shelves with bottles on them. Some bottles are full of different colored liquids and others have powders. In the middle of the room is a large table that has obviously been used regularly for something very mysterious. The markings on the table are fierce and deliberate. Dawn can only imagine in her mind the kind of magic her grandmother, and mother for that matter, conjured up on this table. Most of the concoctions she remembers from the book are intended for different periods of time, but there were a couple of recipes that stuck in her mind as being useful for their journey. One to make someone invisible and one to make someone visible again. The book says that once invisible, there are side effects a person will experience. Their physical strength will be restricted or inhibited. So, it won't be helpful to be invisible when fighting the soldiers; only to quietly hide from them.

Dawn searches through the bottles on the shelves to acquire all the necessary ingredients to make the potions. She will start with the invisible potion first. As she finds each ingredient, she places it on the large table. After she has found everything she will need, she looks for a small, empty bottle with a tight-fitting lid. She finds a drawer full in a cabinet under the table. She takes some out and sets them aside on the table. She finds a mixing bowl in the far corner of the table with a wooden spoon inside. She moves the bowl and spoon to the center of the table where the potion ingredients await. From memory, she begins to place drops of this and capfuls of that into the bowl. Once she is sure she has included everything from the recipe, she stirs the concoction and places it into two of the small bottles. She will use one for testing; and, if it works, the other for their journey. She wipes the bowl with a rag and continues making the other potion. When she is done and has two bottles of each potion, she puts them in a small basket she finds to carry them upstairs. With Zac close behind, they make their way back up the stairs. They lock the door, replace the potato bin, and exit into the kitchen. There is still no one in the kitchen, so they won't have to make excuses as to their interest in the pantry.

Once outside the kitchen and into the main hallway, Dawn mulls around in her mind who should be the lucky one to test her two concoctions. She looks over at Zac.

"Oh, no," Zac says obviously reading her mind, "Not that I don't trust you, but..."

"That's okay," Dawn says with a laugh, "It would be my luck that I switched the recipes, and this potion would turn you into a donkey."

"Yes," Zac says, "That is my fear, as well."

"Bessie," Dawn says, "Bessie will do it."

"Bessie?" Zac inquires, "Who is Bessie?"

"You haven't met my family from the United States," Dawn replies.

"You brought someone with you?" Zac asks again even more puzzled. "Is Bessie a daughter?"

"No, silly," Dawn responds, "Bessie is my cat, and Angus is my bird."

Looking relieved, Zac sighs loudly as he continues to follow Dawn down the hallway. When they reach the room where Bessie and Angus have been housed these three months,

Dawn opens the door and pulls Zac in behind her. Angus is chirping away on his perch, but Dawn doesn't see Bessie in her usual place on the settee.

"Bessie," Dawn says as she looks around the room anticipating Bessie's eagerness to see her.

Bessie walks slowly from under a writing desk but stops to stretch. Dawn and Zac seat themselves on the settee while waiting for Bessie to complete her sleep-recovery ritual. Dawn grabs the leash from the table next to the settee and clips it to Bessie's collar when she finally jumps on Dawn's lap. Dawn strokes her vigorously and introduces her to Zac. Zac reaches over to pet her; and the very smart cat that she is, Bessie takes to Zac right away. Dawn grabs one of the bottles marked 'Invisible' from her basket. She opens it and pours the appropriate amount for Bessie's size into the lid. She nuzzles it over to Bessie. Bessie begins to lap it up. It must taste pretty good. Within minutes of swallowing the entire amount, Dawn and Zac can see Bessie become transparent. They can see less and less of her until, Viola, she has disappeared. Dawn pulls on the leash to feel any movement. She can hear Bessie 'meow,' and she can feel a tug on the leash; so she knows Bessie is still there. She pulls the other bottle from her basket marked 'Visible.' She pours the same amount and holds it in the general vicinity of Bessie. She can see Bessie's tongue disturb the liquid inside the lid. It, too, must taste good; because it doesn't take Bessie long to empty the lid. As Bessie begins to appear back to normal, Dawn strokes her head to reassure her that everything is alright.

"Well," Zac says, "It appears to work. I never really had any doubts, love."

"Sure you didn't," Dawn says sarcastically.

"Now should we try Angus?" Zac says in hopes of dissuading Dawn from trying to make him her next target.

"No," Dawn replies, "I have other plans for Angus."

When Bessie is back to normal and receives an abundance of hugs and kisses from Dawn, she jumps from the settee and meanders over to her water dish and begins to drink. This will help clean the potion from her system. As Bessie continues drinking, Dawn and Zac exit the room and make their way back to the tech lab. Dawn wants to put the remaining two bottles of potion in the safe. Dawn apprises Aunt Eva and James of the magical potions she has made and outlines the intended uses. Aunt Eva is very excited at the prospect of having more ammunition to defeat the witch.

CHAPTER TWENTY-FIVE

Today is the day of the 'zero hour.' James has determined that this day will end with a full moon. The sun of the day and the full moon at night will provide light for more, successful maneuvering inside the hedge. Aunt Eva has arranged for the entire staff to be away from the estate after breakfast. She and James will be monitoring the entire estate for security as well as providing guidance for Dawn and Zac through the hedge. When breakfast is finished and all the staff has left the estate, Dawn, Zac, Aunt Eva, and James gather in the tech lab. James has activated all the monitors on another table. They will be able to see the entire estate from every camera angle on these monitors. They will track Dawn and Zac using the large, wall monitor. While James is testing and activating the 'ear bugs' that will be used by Dawn and Zac, they are adorning themselves in their new combat gear. Once they have finished dressing, they retreat to the workout room where they collect their weapons. They meet James on the patio outside the workout room who takes them on the ATV to the portal entrance. While Dawn and Zac are arranging their weapons and loading other incidentals into pockets and pouches, James is returning to the tech lab. Once in the tech lab, James begins testing the connectivity of the 'ear bugs.'

"Testing Unit One," James says through his microphone, "Can you hear me?"

"Ten four," Dawn replies after activating her microphone.

"Testing Unit Two," James says again, "Can you hear me?"

"Yes," Zac responds.

"Jolly good," James says anxiously, "When you go through the portal and are definitely inside the hedge, request a call-back. If I hear you, I will respond. If not, I guess you are on your own. So, good luck."

Once Dawn and Zac have everything securely attached, Dawn unzips the front of her jacket and pulls the yellow-stoned necklace out. She will be able to see the portal through this stone, because it is daylight; but she has the blue-stoned necklace in case they must get back through the portal at night.

As Dawn and Zac position themselves in front of the rock used to previously mark the portal, she looks through the stone to see if the portal waves are still visible. She can see them but moves to the left to place herself in the middle of the ripples. She returns the necklace into her jacket and zips it up to her neck. Zac is now next to her. She looks up at Zac and smiles nervously.

"Are you ready?" she asks.

"Yes, I believe so," he responds.

"Okay," she continues, "When I say the magical word, the portal will open; and we can walk through. Once inside, I will say another magical word that will close the portal. Anyway, I think that's how it works."

Both Dawn and Zac look around to make sure they have not forgotten anything. Dawn raises her arms towards the portal waves and extends her fingers.

"Rasperialus," she says loudly and projects her fingers at the portal.

Nothing happens. Dawn looks over at Zac with a puzzled expression on her face.

"Maybe I need to be closer," Dawn says.

She steps inches closer and repeats the magicology while projecting her fingers towards the ripples. Still nothing. She moves so close to the portal that her fingertips are submerged into the ripples. She repeats the magicology again.

The ripples begin to spread from the middle to the opposite sides. Dawn can see trees and bushes on the other side. She quickly walks through the portal. She turns to see if Zac is following. When Zac exits the portal, she can see the same ripples on this side. She faces the portal and again raises her arms and extends her fingertips.

"Sinjoleckis," she says loudly and projects her fingertips just barely inside the portal.

Dawn and Zac watch as the ripples run back together, and the portal to the outside world is closed. They look around to verify James' computerized interpretation of the inside of the hedge. There is grass and trees and bushes. It looks like a forest. There is a sky above the trees, but it is very hazy. There is enough light to allow visibility through the forest for now. Dawn decides to do an 'ear bug' check with James. She is crossing her fingers in hopes that all communication is not lost.

"Sound check, Unit One," Dawn says.

No response. Dawn scrunches her face to indicate her disappointment.

"Sound check, Unit One," Dawn says again.

"This is Mother," James says using the code word for his command center in response to the sound check, "We can hear you, Unit One. How about Unit Two?"

"Sound check, Unit Two," Zac says after hearing James' response.

"We can hear you also, Unit Two," James says obviously delighted, "Try to vocalize what you see so we can coordinate with our grid."

"There are just trees, bushes, and shrubs from where we are," Dawn begins, "We are traveling straight. When we reach what we think is the middle of the hedge, we will evaluate the best direction to proceed. I see a hill in the distance through the trees off to the left. As I recall, that is the direction that Uncle George would have fallen. We probably should go in that direction first to see if we can see Uncle George."

When Dawn and Zac get to the suspected middle of the hedge, Dawn pulls a red ribbon from a zippered pocket in her sleeve. She ties the ribbon around the nearest tree.

"What's that for," Zac asks.

"In case we lose communication with Mother," Dawn replies, "We will know where to turn to get back to the portal."

"Good thinking," he says as he bends down to kiss her, "You are beautiful and intelligent."

Dawn turns left and heads towards the hill. Zac follows along.

"Unit One," James says.

"Yes, Mother, what is it?" Dawn replies.

"There is some activity at the other end of the grid. The splotches are congregating in patches. They must know you are inside the hedge."

"Ten four, Mother," Dawn replies, "Let me know when the splotches begin to move in our direction. We are going to look for Uncle George."

"Jolly good," James says.

Dawn and Zac continue towards the hill. After several minutes, Dawn stops to see a couple of rabbits hop across the path ahead. They continue on and find a small pond. The water is surprisingly clear. As they approach the hill, they can see a pile of rocks that have been strategically stacked. Zac pulls out his pistol while Dawn quietly sneaks up on the rocks. She circles the rocks and finds an opening on the opposite side. She looks inside. She sees leaves and, what looks like, rabbit fur. Just as she is about to return to where Zac is standing, a big blob of tin jumps out from behind a bush. Dawn can hear snarls and growls but nothing that resembles English.

"Is that you, George," Zac says loudly.

An arm extends from the big blob of tin and removes a small piece covering a face.

"Xavier?" George says surprisingly.

"Yes, George," Zac responds, "It's me.

"And who is this with you?" George asks glancing over at Dawn.

"This is your niece, Dawn Hunter," Zac replies.

"Oh, heavens be," George begins to chant, "We are saved. Oh, we are saved."

"Well," Dawn says, "Not quite yet. We just got here. We weren't sure you were even alive. James lost your 'ear bug' signal and thought you might be dead. He's been following body-heat movement at the other end of the hedge. He could see none at this end, so he wasn't sure what happened to you."

"The batteries died in my 'ear bug,'" George reports, "And I covered myself in this tin to prevent anyone inside the hedge from finding me. That probably prevented James from seeing my body heat. I haven't seen anyone, but I have heard some terrible racket coming from the other side. I have been able to survive on small animals and some berries. I get water from the pond, but I would love some tea and crumpets."

"I don't have any crumpets," Dawn says as she unzips a side pocket, "But here is an energy bar that might taste better than rabbits and berries."

Dawn looks at Zac as he returns his pistol to its holster. While George is enjoying the energy bar, Dawn begins walking towards the path they have just made.

"Unit One to Mother," Dawn says after activating her microphone.

"Go ahead, Unit One," James says.

"We have found Uncle George," Dawn replies, "He is alive and appears to be well. Just a little hungry."

"Very good, Unit One," James says happily, "Aunt Eva is joyous over the news."

"We can't take him with us," Dawn advises, "I'm afraid he will slow us down. We will try to get him back to the portal and let him out."

"I'm not sure you're going to have time for that," James replies, "There is a plethora of activity and movement at the other end of the hedge. You need to proceed immediately in that direction."

"We will leave Uncle George here in hiding then and pick him up on our way out," Dawn says.

Dawn extracts a couple more energy bars from her pocket and gives them to Uncle George.

"Wait here, Uncle George, and keep hidden," Dawn instructs, "We will return for you."

Dawn glances at Zac and motions with her hand to indicate they will be backtracking through the trees. When they have gone a considerable distance, Dawn stops and begins to retrieve something from her side pouch. Zac stops at her side wondering what she is doing. As Dawn pulls Angus from her pouch, Zac begins to laugh.

"I wasn't enough company for you, my dear?" Zac inquires.

"You are absolutely enough company," Dawn replies, "You're just not small enough."

Dawn holds Angus in her left hand as she prepares her right hand to generate magical energy and begins to chant:

"Little Angus, you will be,
A lofty eagle with eyes to see,
What lies ahead for us to know,
The dangers wreaking down below."

Magical energy bolts from her fingers into Angus, and he begins to transform into the lofty eagle Dawn has commanded. Once the transformation is complete, Dawn tosses Angus into the air. Both Dawn and Zac watch as Angus ascends into the air and begins to fly ahead. Dawn closes her eyes to see what Angus is seeing as he flies over the terrain. She can see treetops and sporadic patches of green grass. Suddenly, there are no longer any trees; just a clearing of green grass. As Angus soars across the clearing, Dawn can see more trees but smaller and much less dense. In the trees she sees the tops of what looks like wooden roofs; small bunkers forming a circle around a fire. There are some soldiers sitting around the fire, and some milling around the bunkers. They look as if they are preparing for something. Angus continues his journey towards the opposite side of the hedge. As he approaches the end, he displays the vision of a large, castle-like structure. Dawn suspects this is where the witch is. She has made herself a nice, large home over the past twenty-five years.

Sensing he cannot go any further in that direction, Angus turns to travel parallel to the end of the hedge behind the castle. Dawn can see soldiers gathering weapons and making their way to the front of the structure. Before Angus reaches the other side of the hedge, he turns to make his way back to Dawn. He shows Dawn another campsite of soldiers on this side of the hedge. They are flashing swords and forming marching lines.

Dawn opens her eyes and sees Angus flying directly towards her. She holds up her arm for his perch.

"Undunosis," she says as Angus turns back into her cute, little canary.

As she puts Angus back into a pouch, she begins to brief Zac and Mother on the lay of the land.

"Mother, this is Unit One," Dawn says as she activates her 'ear bug.'

"Go ahead, Unit One," James replies.

"At the end of these trees," Dawn begins, "There is a clearing of grass; then, more trees but not as thick. In those trees on each side of the hedge, there are two groups of soldiers. James, can you see splotches in the areas I have just described?"

"Yes," James replies, "There are five splotches in the area to your right. Back farther to your left, there are six splotches."

"Okay," Dawn continues, "At the far end of the hedge, there is a castle-like structure which is surrounded by soldiers. Can you see the structure?"

"I can see splotches," James says, "In a circular formation. I can't see a structure, but the formation would indicate they are surrounding something. If the witch is inside the structure, I don't have visibility of her."

"Very well," Dawn replies, "This is the plan. Since they will obviously see us coming across the clearing, Zac and I will drink the invisibility potion. Once we have reached sufficient cover, we will incarnate ourselves using the other potion and attack the soldiers on the right. I will report back when this plan is accomplished. Over and out."

Both Dawn and Zac deactivate their 'ear bugs' and continue their journey towards the clearing.

CHAPTER TWENTY-SIX

About an hour later, Dawn can see hazy sky ahead through the last of the trees. Dawn assumes they will reach the clearing in just minutes. As they approach the last of the trees, Dawn is perplexed to still see hazy sky; not the green grass clearing she saw when Angus flew over it. When they get closer, Dawn takes a step out to exit the trees but begins to slide down. Zac grabs one of her straps wrapped around her back to prevent her from falling down a huge drop. Dawn and Zac retreat backwards a few steps to regain balance and composure but inch themselves forward again to look down at the clearing below. The drop looks like about fifty feet. This must be the barrier that James saw on the grid.

Zac extracts a rope from his backpack and ties it to one of the last trees. Since they won't be able to use any magical powers while they are invisible, Dawn and Zac decide to wait to drink the potion until they are in the clearing. Zac goes first. He descends the rope and holds the bottom for Dawn. Once they are both safely down, Dawn pulls the bottle of invisibility potion from one of her pouches. She pours a capful for Zac and waits while he drinks it. Seeing the results are successful, she pours a second capful and quickly drinks it herself. She replaces the bottle of potion into her pouch and waits just seconds. When Zac's image becomes fuzzy, Dawn knows they are both invisible.

"Let's make our way across the clearing," Dawn says, "We need to be as quiet as possible. As we get closer to the other trees, we should be able to see the campfire.

We will find an adequate hiding place and drink the other potion. If all goes well, we should be able to sneak up on the soldiers. James said there are five of them. You take two, and I'll take three."

"How come you get three?" Zac inquires.

"Because I'm going to kill the first two with my bow and arrows," Dawn replies with a sheepish smile, "And the third with my sword, while you are trying to kill two with your sword. But don't worry. If you get into trouble, I will help with your two."

Dawn begins to quietly jog across the clearing. Zac follows close behind. As Dawn predicted, they can see the campfire through the next set of trees. She leads Zac to a big cluster of bushes where she determines it is safe to hide. Before entering the cluster, she looks around to make sure no one is around to witness their transformation. Once inside, Dawn pulls the other bottle of potion from her pouch. This time, she takes the first capful. She quickly refills the cap and gives it to Zac. When her vision of Zac is no longer fuzzy, she knows their visibility has been restored.

"Well, that was relatively painless," Zac jokes.

"Next time, I will see if I can add something spicy," Dawn replies, "So you won't be disappointed."

"You're all the spice I can handle, thank you," Zac says.

Just then, they can hear some rustling outside the cluster. Zac lies down on his belly and scoots himself through the bottom of the bush to get a glimpse of boots walking past. He places his index finger against his lips to indicate silence. Dawn grabs her bow from her shoulder and jumps from the bushes. The soldier that just passed hears the rustling of the leaves and turns around. He sees Dawn and grabs his sword but not before she extracts an arrow from her quiver, places it into the site, and aims the point at the soldier. As he walks towards her, Dawn lets go of the bow string and watches as the arrow whistles through the air. The arrow hits the soldier in the neck. Blood spurts from the wound while Dawn grabs another arrow and walks towards the soldier. Upon approach, Dawn can see the soldier withering up into a furry ball.

In the meantime, Zac is making his way from the bushes. He follows Dawn to see the end result of her attack. He picks up the arrow with a furry pelt attached.

"It looks like a dead rabbit," Zac whispers, "James is right. The witch has been using her magic to turn varmints into soldiers."

He tosses the arrow and pelt into the nearby trees and stares at Dawn who looks rather pleased with herself.

"Okay, one down, four to go," she says.

"Is that two for me and two for you," Zac replies sarcastically, "Or do you still get three?"

Dawn rolls her eyes as she returns the second arrow back into her quiver and begins walking towards the distant campfire. Zac follows with his sword at the ready. As they approach the campfire, Dawn veers off to the right and motions for Zac to go to the left. Dawn loads her bow with an arrow and begins walking quickly towards her first target. Again, the arrow whistles through the air alerting the soldiers to their presence. The arrow hits one of the soldiers but bounces off his leather chest protector. Dawn releases another arrow that lands just under the protector penetrating the stomach. The soldier goes down but is still alive. One more time, Dawn sends an arrow at the soldier hitting him sideways through the sleeve of the protector into his heart. This soldier, too, withers into a furry ball.

Dawn sees that Zac is now approaching two of the soldiers with sword drawn in attack mode. She extracts her sword and walks to the awaiting soldier. The soldier lifts his sword to attack Dawn as she approaches. As the soldier swings his sword down to project a blow to her head, Dawn stops the motion with her own sword. When the soldier backs up to maintain his balance, Dawn strikes him from behind. As Dawn turns to strike again, she sees only a shriveled blob of fur. Dawn looks over to see how Zac is progressing with his assignment. Zac is orchestrating his final blow to the last of the soldiers in this section. While Zac is composing himself after his battle, Dawn is checking in with Mother to get bearings on the next area.

"This is Unit One," Dawn says activating her microphone, "Do you copy?"

"Yes, Unit One," James responds, "You must have terminated the soldiers in that section, because the splotches have disappeared from the grid."

"Yes," Dawn reports, "What does the next area look like?"

"There are six splotches moving in your direction," James says.

"Ten, four," Dawn replies, "We'll meet them halfway."

"Six soldiers," Zac inquires with a smile, "Does that mean three for you and three for me?"

"That sounds right," Dawn replies.

"Finally, a fair fight," Zac says.

Sword in hand, Zac takes the lead. Dawn follows behind loading her bow with an arrow. As Dawn sees the soldiers within shooting distance, she propels three arrows, one after another. Each arrow hits their mark, and three soldiers turn into fur. Leaving three soldiers, Zac attacks two soldiers while Dawn readies her sword for one. As the battle ends, Dawn and Zac are again victorious.

Checking in with Mother, they discover there are eight splotches fencing the front of the structure which is about a mile away. James doesn't believe that any of these splotches are the witch. There is not enough heat projecting from the splotches to equal the witch's energy. Because James cannot see any heat indicators coming from the structure, he concludes the structure is made of something that is blocking any energy signals. Therefore, he can't predict who or how many are inside the structure. Once the soldiers outside the structure have been eliminated, Dawn and Zac will have to investigate inside blindly, so to speak. Dawn and Zac move on to the next battle of eight.

As Dawn gauges their travel speed, she determines they are very close to the structure. She retrieves a small set of binoculars from one of her pouches and stops to view what's ahead. Through the lenses, she can see the roof of a very tall castle. As she pans back and forth, she gets an idea of the size of the castle. When she reaches the foundation of the structure, she can see the eight soldiers guarding the front. She estimates it will take another half-hour to reach their next battle.

"Let's rest here for a while," Dawn says to Zac as she begins to discard weapons from her body.

Zac does the same but hangs on to his sword as they both seat themselves in the grass next to a large tree. Dawn removes the lid from a canteen and begins to drink. She hands the canteen to Zac. He, too, drinks. Once refreshed, they begin to plan their attack. As Dawn talks about eliminating as many of the soldiers with her bow and arrow, Zac checks his pistol to make sure all the chambers contain a bullet. He has six of them. Just as he is replacing his pistol into the holster, they can hear some movement in the nearby grass. They can't see anything, but they can see the grass move.

"Cleeridundum," Dawn whispers as she projects her hand towards the moving grass.

Dawn can see the outline of someone in a long cloak. She grabs her bow and loads it with an arrow. She points it towards the outline and shoots. She misses the outline but retrieves another arrow for a second shot. When she tries to aim more accurately this time, she realizes the outline is gone. She lowers her bow in disappointment.

"What was that all about?" Zac inquires.

"I think it was the witch," Dawn replies, "She made herself invisible. I was able to cast a spell to outline her form. She has, however, escaped. She won't return now she knows I can see her outline. If you're ready, let's move on."

Dawn and Zac collect their weapons and gear and begin walking towards the castle.

When they are within shooting distance, they prepare for battle; Dawn with her bow and arrows, and Zac with his pistol. As the soldiers see Dawn and Zac approaching, they pull their swords and begin marching to attack. Dawn on one side and Zac on the other, they both begin shooting. Dawn downs three soldiers with her arrows while Zac downs two using five of his six bullets. Three soldiers are left. In an attempt to even the odds, Zac fires his last bullet. He hits one of the soldiers in the arm but only grazes him. Dawn has pulled her sword and is running an attack. Zac, too, pulls his sword to thwart the attack of the oncoming wounded soldier. As Dawn eliminates one more soldier, she turns just in time to see another soldier heading in her direction swinging his sword. Before the soldier has a chance to complete the downward motion of his sword, Dawn injects the tip of her sword into his chest. The blow is fatal, and the soldier withers away. Pulling her sword from the fur ball, Dawn lifts her sword in combat position to be ready for the next battle. She looks around but sees nothing; no one. Not even Zac.

"Zac," she yells, "Where are you?"

"I'm here," Zac whispers almost inaudibly.

"Where?" Dawn asks again as she runs in the direction of his last known sighting.

Zac raises his sword just enough for Dawn to discover his whereabouts. She runs to him. She can see that he has been wounded. A sword blow to the arm. His fighting arm, at that. She kneels down beside him and tries to stop the bleeding by pressurizing the wound with her hand. With her other hand, she pulls a bandage from her pouch. She ties the bandage around the wound but can see that blood is still leaking through.

"We need to get you back," Dawn says.

"No," Zac responds, "You need to kill the witch."

"There is still time," Dawn replies, "It is getting dark anyway. I can see the moon in the hazy sky. It will give us enough light to return to the portal. I can come back in the morning."

With that, Dawn stands and grabs Zac's other arm to help him to his feet. As fast as Zac can travel in his condition, they make their way back to the portal. They travel quickly through the trees and across the grass clearing. When they reach the fifty-foot wall, Dawn realizes Zac is getting weaker and is not going to be able to pull himself up the rope. Dawn decides to ascend the rope first. Knowing she doesn't have the strength to pull Zac up the wall, she will use her magic. Once she has safely arrived at the top of the wall, she looks down and advises Zac to securely attach himself to the rope.

"Upanwayonus," Dawn says as she holds the rope.

The rope begins to move into a pile next to the tree where Zac had previously attached it. Dawn waits on her knees at the top of the wall as the rope inches Zac closer and closer to her. When Zac has reached the top and Dawn has secured his safety, she wraps his arm around her neck and assists him towards the portal. As they reach the tree with the red ribbon Dawn used to identify the location of the portal, she helps Zac seat himself on a nearby rock.

"Wait here and rest," Dawn instructs, "I'm going to get Uncle George. I will need his help getting you through the portal."

Dawn realizes she should contact Mother to report Zac's injury. They need to have a doctor waiting. He has lost a lot of blood and appears to be very weak.

"Mother, this is Unit One," Dawn says after activating her microphone, "Come in, Mother."

"This is Mother," James replies, "Where are you? I only see one big splotch towards the left side of the grid; just up from the portal."

"That would be me and Zac," Dawn says, "I'm not sure how much body heat he is generating because he has been injured and has lost a lot of blood. He will need a doctor. I am going to go get Uncle George so he can help me carry Zac through the portal."

"Oh, blimey," James gasps, "We will send for the doctor right away."

"Ten, four, over and out," Dawn says.

Dawn turns towards the hill she can see in the distance. She doesn't travel far when she sees Uncle George running towards her.

"I could hear your transmission," Uncle George says.

"Quick," Dawn replies, "Zac is injured. I need your help getting him through the portal."

Both Dawn and Uncle George return to where Zac is seated. He is wobbling back and forth as if drifting in and out of consciousness. Dawn grabs him from one side while Uncle George grabs him from the other. Zac is trying to walk on his own as much as possible; but with the blood loss, his efforts aren't much help. When they reach the end of the trees, Dawn unzips her jacket to retrieve the blue-stoned pendant. She turns it over and looks through the stone. She moves the stone around and around, up and down. She finally sees the start of the ripples off to the right.

"This way, Uncle George," she says as she walks to the right.

With Zac in between, Uncle George moves in the same direction. Still holding the stone up in front of her face, she glances again into it. She can see the ripples of the portal very clearly. She drops the necklace and reaches out to touch the ripples as close to the middle as possible.

"Rasperialis," Dawn shouts with fingertips from one hand inside the ripples.

The portal opens. Dawn and Uncle George secure Zac between them and walk quickly through the portal. James and Aunt Eva are waiting as all three clear the portal. James quickly grabs Zac from Dawn as she hurriedly tries to shut the portal.

"Sinjoleckis," Dawn says as the portal closes.

She turns back towards Zac to help with his treatment. James and Uncle George are loading him onto the back seat of an ATV when another ATV appears from behind.

"Doctor Bailey," James shouts out to the driver of the second ATV, "Come with me in this ATV. We need to get Zac to the house for medical treatment."

Dr. Bailey exits the ATV and seats himself in the back seat next to Zac. He tries to examine Zac's arm as James hurriedly drives back to the house. After some welcoming hugs from Aunt Eva, Uncle George helps her into the second ATV. Dawn plants herself in the driver's seat and encourages both Aunt Eva and Uncle George to save their 'welcome home' ritual for later. Dawn follows the first ATV back to the house. Dr. Bailey left two nurses and a gurney on the patio in preparation for Zac's arrival. James and Dr. Bailey help a semi-conscious Zac on the gurney. The two nurses wheel the gurney across the patio, through the double doors, and down the hallway into a spare bedroom as Dr. Bailey follows. James awaits the arrival of the second ATV to assist with Aunt Eva. He knows Dawn will want to move quickly to be with Zac. As Dawn makes her way across the patio and disappears inside the house, James takes a moment to examine Uncle George.

"Well, George," James says, "You don't look any worse for the wear."

"Maybe not," George replies, "But I could jolly well use a cup of tea and some crumpets."

All three of them laugh as James wheels Aunt Eva across the patio with George at her side. They enter the house and make their way directly to the spare bedroom where they know Zac is in good hands. Dr. Bailey is the most highly regarded doctor in England, and he happens to be a close neighbor. Zac has already been made comfortable on the bed, and IVs have been installed. Dr. Bailey is examining Zac's wound as Aunt Eva, James, and George enter the room. Dawn is standing at the foot of the bed looking on with deep concern.

"Will he be okay, doctor?" Dawn asks fighting back tears.

"The wound doesn't look too bad," the doctor reports, "But he has lost a lot of blood which has made him weak. It will take a few days for his body to regenerate his blood, but he should be alright."

Dawn sighs with relief as Aunt Eva reaches for her hand and gives it a squeeze.

"And how are you doing, my dear?" Aunt Eva inquires.

"I'm fine. Just a little tired," Dawn replies.

"Well, I am so glad it is over," James says happily.

"Oh," Dawn says, "It is not over."

Both James and Aunt Eva look puzzled as Dawn explains that the witch is still alive. Because of Zac's injuries, they had to leave before she had a chance to enter the castle and confront the witch.

"Oh, dear," James says somewhat deflated, "I didn't see any more splotches but yours, so I assumed everyone was dead."

"No," Dawn replies, "The witch is inside the castle; and, you were right. The material used for the roof is blocking any heat or energy from reaching your sensors. I believe the witch is alone in there. If she had soldiers inside, she would have sent them out after we eliminated the soldiers guarding the front of her castle. In any event, I will be going back in tomorrow. It will be she and I. Mano-a-mano."

CHAPTER TWENTY-SEVEN

Dawn checks on Zac before retiring for the evening. He is asleep, but she takes the opportunity to look at him. She is so grateful that he is not hurt worse. He will have a memorable scar on his arm; but as he said earlier, it shows character as if he needs a scar to determine his character. After about thirty minutes, Dawn kisses Zac on his forehead and retreats to her room.

After showering and dressing in her pajamas, Dawn lies on top of the comforter with her head on one of the many pillows arranged around the bed. She is very tired, both physically and mentally. As she looks up at the ceiling, she feels herself drifting off.

Just as she is about to drift into a very deep sleep, she opens her eyes to see her mother sitting on the edge of the bed as she had done once before. She takes Dawn's hand and cups it into both of hers. Dawn can feel a tingling move from the hand her mother is holding, up her arm, across her shoulders, and down the other arm and hand. Her mother tells her that she is transferring magical energy into her body to ensure that Dawn has all the powers she was promised in the family legacy. Her mother also tells her that she should take the book into the hedge with her. The book contains not only magical writings but also magical energy stored there throughout the many years as it moved from generation to generation. She assures Dawn that she will be with her throughout her journey and subsequent battle.

Dawn arises especially refreshed and invigorated. She doesn't waste any time preparing for the day. She wants to check on Zac and spend as much time with him as possible before she again enters the hedge. She quickly dresses in her black tights and knit shirt knowing she will adorn her combat gear in the tech lab. She goes to the spare bedroom on the main floor where Zac is hopefully resting peacefully. The doctor has stitched and treated his wound and provided appropriate medication. As she enters the room, she sees Zac is sitting up while a nurse is rewrapping his arm bandage. Dawn inches closer to the bed as the nurse completes her medical duties. Zac looks up to see Dawn approaching most gingerly. His face lights up when she reaches the bed and grabs the hand of his 'good' arm. She cups his hand into both of hers and rubs her cheek against the top of it. A tear falls from her eye, and Zac can feel the warm wetness on his hand. He pulls her hands away from her cheek and kisses them both.

Wiping more tears from her cheek, Dawn says sarcastically, "Boy, some guys will do anything not to have a repeat date."

"Oh, my dear, don't you worry," Zac replies reassuringly, "There will be a repeat date when you return. I've helped all I can. I know that. You have to do the rest on your own."

Dawn nods and squeezes his hand tightly. Just as she is about to lean across the bed to kiss him, Chumley enters the room.

"Miss Hunter, Madam Ninsky wishes to see you in the tech lab," Chumley says.

"Okay," Dawn replies, "Tell her I'll be right there."

Dawn looks over at Zac and throws him a kiss with her lips as she walks towards the door. She leaves the bedroom and makes her way to the tech lab. As James opens and relocks both doors in the tech lab to allow her entrance, Dawn can hear Aunt Eva and Uncle George discussing something rather peculiar. All the servants were told that Uncle George had gone on a business trip. Apparently, no one gave that excuse a second thought; except, Ms. Johnson. Uncle George is telling Aunt Eva about the 'third degree' he got this morning from Ms. Johnson. As Dawn approaches the table where they are sitting, Aunt Eva greets her with a smile and begins to brief her on the day's schedule.

"Without giving all the servants another day off and making them suspicious," Aunt Eva explains, "I have scheduled a time this morning when no one will have visibility of the hedge and the portal. You will be able to enter the portal without being noticed. James, George, and I will reroute and reschedule today's activities to avoid anyone being in that area at all during the day. Since we don't know when you will return through the portal, we will try to keep the area clear. With the 'ear bug' communication system working so brilliantly, we should be able to gauge your whereabouts and monitor the portal accordingly."

Dawn nods and looks up at the large monitor on the wall. For the first time, the grid is clear; no splotches. A chill goes through her body. She realizes she will be inside that grid alone with the witch. She tells Aunt Eva and James about her dream. She tells them she will be taking the book with her into the hedge; but in the meantime she will study up on her magicology. While Aunt Eva and Uncle George are planning to brief the servants on their assignments for the day, she asks James to open the safe and retrieve the book. She remembers some older magic at the front of the book she quickly expunged as being too old for her needs. After her experience inside the hedge and the advice her mother gave her in her dream, she is now confident some of the older magic may be useful. As James reprograms the grid based on information he obtained from Dawn and Zac when they returned, she spends some time thoroughly studying the parts of the book she had previously overlooked. When she has sufficiently filled her brain with more magicology, she has James replace the book into the safe until she is ready to leave. She decides she will transport the book in a backpack. Since this battle will involve mostly magic, she will not be taking any weapons.

Dawn leaves the tech lab knowing she has about an hour before she will re-enter the portal. She wants to spend these moments with Zac in case they are her last. She makes her way to the bedroom where Zac is recovering. As she enters, she sees Zac trying to eat some lunch using his other hand. He awkwardly tries to find his mouth with the fork. Some of the food on the fork reaches his mouth, while some of it falls down his shirt. He is a far-cry from the ravenous diner he usually is during mealtime. Zac looks up and sees Dawn enter the room. He places his fork back on the bed tray and pushes it aside. He smiles widely as Dawn approaches. She seats herself on the bed next to him and maneuvers around to lie at his side. Using his good arm, of course, he puts it around her neck allowing her head to rest on his shoulder.

"I feel just terrible that you are going back into the hedge alone," Zac says.

"Oh, don't worry," Dawn replies, "I'm not going in alone."

Zac lifts his arm to alert Dawn she needs to sit facing him.

"You have found a new boyfriend already?" Zac inquires jealously.

"No, nothing like that," Dawn replies, "I'm taking Bessie."

"Bessie?" Zac says surprisingly, "I'm being replaced by a cat? A small one, at that. How helpful is she going to be?"

"Oh, you'd be surprised," Dawn says, "Just imagine a large, Bengal tiger at my side as we walk through that grassy clearing towards the castle. It came to me earlier this morning. I was going through some old magicology and found some spells that will be most beneficial. It may just be intimidating enough to catch the witch off guard."

After careful consideration and consolation that he is still her 'main man,' Zac agrees with Dawn. He grabs her arm and pulls her close. He kisses her gently again and again; on her lips and all over her face. She relishes in the attention and romantic tenderness. She tries to clear her mind of any impending doom and gloom by clinging to Zac as long as possible. Her desire to stay with Zac is short-lived as Chumley enters the room to deliver a message from Aunt Eva.

"Your aunt is asking for you, Miss Hunter," Chumley says.

"Thank you, Chumley," Dawn replies, "I will be right there."

Dawn waits for Chumley to leave the room, and she leans over Zac's bed to give him a 'goodbye' kiss. It is long but soft and gentle. As she backs away from the bed, she clings to his arm until she reaches his fingertips with hers. She turns and walks to the door, throwing him another kiss as she leaves.

As she enters the tech lab, she can see that everyone is there and in their places. Uncle George hands Dawn her 'ear bug' for a test while James is scrolling through different grids on the main monitor to track any activity at all. When it is determined that all electronics are working properly, Dawn begins to install her gear. Once everything is arranged into pockets and pouches, Dawn waits to put on her backpack until James has removed the book from the safe. She puts the book into an inside partition of the backpack and zips it before securing it to her back and clipping the straps around her front. Dawn double-checks to see that she has both pendants around her neck. Once assured, she zips her leather jacket clear to the top.

"It's time, my dear," Aunt Eva says, "George will be taking you to the portal. So as not to draw any attention, he will drop you off and immediately return. Good luck and take our love with you."

Dawn bends down to hug Aunt Eva. She walks over to the desk and gives James a hug as well. She sees Aunt Eva wipe away a tear as she leaves the tech lab. Uncle George follows her down the stairway. When they reach the main hallway, Dawn takes a detour to the room where Bessie and Angus are housed. Bessie is outstretched on the settee as usual and has no idea she is about to earn her keep. Dawn quickly walks over and picks Bessie up in her arms. She tucks her under her arm on top of a pouch and secures her with a strap. Uncle George looks confused but follows close behind as they walk outside the double doors onto the patio. The ATV is waiting at the edge as both Dawn and Uncle George seat themselves in front. Uncle George quickly drives Dawn to the portal looking around the entire way making sure no one is watching. When they reach the portal, Dawn jumps out and hugs Uncle George.

"Goodbye," Uncle George says, "Hurry back. We will be waiting."

Uncle George quickly pulls away. Dawn watches as he returns to the house. When he is out of sight, she pulls the yellow-stoned pendant from around her neck. She checks Bessie and all her gear before looking around one last time. When all is clear, she lifts the pendant to her eyes and looks for the ripples. She sees them and quickly adjusts herself to ensure her placement in the center of the ripples. She reaches out her fingers and can feel the ripples on the tips.

"Rasperialus," she says.

The portal begins to open. She is getting much better at this. She returns the pendant inside her jacket and walks through the portal. Once on the other side, she turns to close the portal.

"Sinjoleckis," she says and watches as the portal closes.

CHAPTER TWENTY-EIGHT

Dawn begins to walk through the trodden grass to the middle. She can still see footprints that she and Zac made on their way out the day before. She follows the footprints for about an hour until she comes to the barrier drop. The rope is still curled up into a pile next to the tree; however, she won't be using it. It is magic all the way this time.

"Propelaronga," Dawn says as she steps off the edge of the wall and slowly lands in the grassy clearing below.

Once she has secured her footing, she unstraps Bessie from under her arm. She sets her down on the ground and steps back slightly to make room for the impending visitor. She chants as she forms small circles with both arms pointing them at Bessie:

"My furry cat so loyal and true,
A magic spell I cast on you,
A Bengal tiger you will be,
And by my side to escort me."

Dawn watches as Bessie makes the magical transformation into the biggest Bengal tiger she has ever seen. Not that she has seen that many, but this magical tiger seems to outdo her own imagination. Bessie roars to indicate her possible approval of her new 'digs' as Dawn begins to walk across the grassy clearing.

Separated by about ten feet, Bessie walks on one side down the middle of the clearing; and Dawn walks on the other. Bessie is on her left, but Dawn feels a strong presence of someone on her right. For a moment as the sun filters through the hazy sky, Dawn thinks she sees the image of her mother walking simultaneously across the clearing. She has an inner sense of peace. When she reaches the trees at the end of the clearing, Dawn can see that Bessie has disappeared into the bushes. She can hear rustling but can't see her. She proceeds straight ahead confident that Bessie is also moving forward. Off to the right, she sees the first campfire she and Zac encountered the day before. She no longer sees her mother but knows she is still with her. Further ahead she sees a stream of smoke on the left from the second campfire. She is now about a mile from the castle. She continues on her journey glancing over to assure herself that Bessie is still traveling at an equal pace. She reaches the end of the trees and sees the castle a stones-throw away. She doesn't see Bessie but hopes she will follow along shortly.

Dawn walks slowly from the trees onto a narrow wooden bridge that leads to a door. There is no lock on the door, just a latch. She lifts the latch and pushes the door open. It squeaks loudly and slams shut behind her as she enters. She looks around to see if the noise has disturbed anyone or anything. It seems to be rather academic anyway, because she is sure the witch knows she is there. It is just a matter of trying to be prepared for any sudden attack.

There is a large, arena-type opening inside the door with a stairway at the far end. Dawn can see the entire second level from the middle of the arena. She circles completely around to view the entire foundation. From the corner of her eye, Dawn can see a shadow walking between columns on the second level. She prepares herself for an impending attack. Expecting to be taken by surprise, she is quite befuddled when the witch comes strolling down the stairs and into the arena.

"You're not Hilda," the witch says, "Who are you?"

Wondering what this verbal exchange is going to accomplish, Dawn says nothing as she walks towards the witch.

"I said," the witch repeats, "Who are you?"

"I am Hilda's daughter," Dawn finally says.

"Where is Hilda?" the witch inquires.

"She is unavailable," Dawn replies, "You will have to deal with me."

"So be it," the witch says as she thrusts a web of energy directly at Dawn.

Dawn is thrown across the arena into the dirt.

"This is going to be fun," the witch cackles, "Your mother will be sorry she didn't come."

"I don't think so," Dawn replies as she walks swiftly back to the center of the arena.

As she walks she is rotating both arms to conjure up the biggest ball of energy she can. She projects the sphere directly at the witch with as much thrust as she has ever used before. The witch raises her arms to deflect the sphere but underestimates the power that Dawn possesses. The witch is tossed against the rock wall behind her.

"Not so much fun now, hey?" Dawn says sarcastically.

The witch catches her breath and decides to change her tactics. Dawn seems to be a more worthy opponent than she had anticipated.

Calculating the levels of magical power Dawn possesses, the witch realizes Dawn may have an extra level on her side. The witch decides to allow Dawn several more strikes. This will deplete her magical energy, giving the witch the advantage. The witch moves away from the wall allowing Dawn to attack several more times. Dawn can feel herself weakening from the intensity of her thrusting. As the witch positions herself to finally make a counterattack, Dawn finds herself too drained to conjure up a defense. The witch orchestrates sufficient power to levitate Dawn into the air and project her through the columns and into the wall on the second level of the castle. Not wanting to waste her energy to levitate herself to the second level, the witch decides to take the stairs.

As she rounds the corner to the upper level section where Dawn is lying on her back on the ground frantically trying to catch her breath, the witch can see that Dawn is weakening by the minute. Since she, too, is losing energy with every projectile, she walks towards Dawn to finish her off. Just as she is about to release the fatal thrust at Dawn, Bessie roars loudly and attacks the witch from behind. The witch must use her energy to thwart the intentions of the large, Bengal tiger by levitating herself to the arena below. She hates to give Dawn too much time to rejuvenate her powers; but she needs time to redirect her powers as well. Bessie watches over Dawn as she slowly begins to recover. Dawn sits up and scoots herself back against the rock wall. She sends Bessie down to the arena to keep the witch at bay until she can extract all possible power from the book.

While Bessie is roaring and growling and clawing at the witch, Dawn takes the book from her backpack and puts it in her lap. She places both hands on it and begins to chant:

"Oh, mighty powers come to me,
Infiltrate my hands to see,
That all the powers contained herein,
Will help command this war to win."

Dawn can feel the most intense sensation moving from the book into her fingertips, into her hands, and up her arms. She feels stronger than she ever felt before. She sets the book aside and stands up. She looks over the banister to see that Bessie is moving slowly towards the witch. The witch is obviously rallying her powers to exterminate Bessie. Dawn can see she hasn't enough time to physically walk around the second level to the stairway. She will have to use her powers to levitate down. Using magicology and her newly rejuvenated powers, she propels herself down to the arena and lands between the witch and Bessie just in time to deflect a thrust of magical energy aimed towards Bessie. Bessie retreats to the side of the arena giving Dawn plenty of room to battle the witch.

Dawn can see that the witch is weakening and hopes that her own powers are stable enough to maintain the needed strength to eliminate the witch. Seeing that the witch is rallying her powers, Dawn must act quickly. She closes her eyes and tenses her entire body to pull every ounce of magical energy she has to exact the final blow. As she opens her eyes, she can feel herself lift from the ground. She points both extended arms at the witch and chants:

"Wicked witch, your time is through,
I cast this spell to finish you."

Once she has corralled all the energy
into a bundle, Dawn mightily thrusts her arms
in the direction of the witch as she shouts,
"Hazmadionus."

The electrified bundle flies through the
air and lands right on top of the witch where
it immediately bursts into a large ball of
flames. Dawn can hear the painful cries of
the witch through the flickers of the fire.
When the flames are extinguished by total
elimination of its fuel, Dawn can see nothing
but ashes piled on the ground. From across
the arena, Bessie walks towards Dawn who is
staring victoriously at the remains of the
witch.

"Let's go home, Bessie," Dawn says as she
pets the top of Bessie's head.

They both are fatigued from their battle,
but they will muster enough energy to return
home. Once they have left the castle, Dawn
tries to make contact with Mother. She has no
such luck. She decides to wait until she
reaches the grassy clearing.

After about an hour, Dawn and Bessie
reach the clearing. She decides to wait until
they arrive at the barrier wall to change
Bessie back to her regular self. For now, she
will try again to reach Mother.

"This is Unit One," Dawn says after
activating her microphone, "Come in, Mother.
Can anyone hear me?"

After a moment, James responds most
excitedly, "Yes, Unit One, we can hear you.
Since I am now talking to you, I am assuming
the large flash and flair we saw on the

computer grid was the destruction of the witch. Also, something miraculous has happened. At the very moment of the flash and flair, a small jolt went through Eva. She was able to rise from her wheelchair and walk around the tech lab. The witch's spell has been broken."

"That is wonderful," Dawn replies, "We're coming home. See you soon."

Feeling very accomplished, Dawn continues her journey across the clearing with Bessie by her side. Meanwhile, a celebration of Aunt Eva's good fortune is taking place in the tech lab. James and Eva are dancing and circling the tech lab. They get so wrapped up in their frivolity that Aunt Eva gets tangled in the computer cords. She falls to the floor as James rushes to save her from injury. James falls to the floor as well. They both look at each other and begin to laugh loudly. It is the noise of Eva's elevator that quickly brings them back to their senses. James arises and helps Eva stand. As they both brush themselves off and make sure all is well, they look up to see George exit the elevator with Ms. Johnson close behind.

"George?" Eva says surprisingly, "What is Nancy doing here?"

As George and Ms. Johnson approach the middle of the tech lab where Eva and James are standing, they can see that Ms. Johnson has a gun jammed into George's back.

"How is it that you are walking?" Ms. Johnson asks directing her question to Eva.

"Well, a family prophecy has been fulfilled," Eva says without giving any more specific information.

"It has something to do with the book, doesn't it?" Ms. Johnson inquires. Before Eva can respond, Ms. Johnson continues, "That's why I am here. I want that book. Where is it?"

"Well," Eva says very hesitantly, "Dawn has it."

"And where is she?" Ms. Johnson asks.

To tell Ms. Johnson where Dawn is, she will have to tell her about the hedge. She is in a very precarious situation. George has a gun in his back, and there is every indication that Ms. Johnson is serious enough to shoot him. Eva has no choice; she must divulge the family secret.

"Dawn is inside the hedge," Eva says.

"And that, I guess, is part of the prophecy as well," Ms. Johnson says anxiously, "It makes sense now. Everything must be in that book. I am more determined than ever to get my hands on that book. I know you have been communicating with Dawn. When will she be exiting the hedge?"

Eva hesitates as she moves closer to the computer to covertly try to disconnect visibility of the grid. They can still see two small splotches moving across the middle of the grid which indicates Dawn's whereabouts inside the hedge. Realizing her intent, Ms. Johnson quickly diverts Eva's actions by jamming the gun deeper into George's back. When George winces, Eva changes her plan of action.

Ms. Johnson looks up at the grid. She now knows that the splotches on the grid must be the electronic means to monitor Dawn's movements inside the hedge.

"Where will Dawn be exiting the hedge?" Ms. Johnson asks.

Knowing they are not going to be able to lie or otherwise try to fool Ms. Johnson, Eva has no choice but to honestly answer her questions.

"There is a portal about here," Eva replies as she points to a place on the grid where the portal approximates.

"Well," Ms. Johnson responds feeling most achieved, "We will be greeting her at the portal."

Ms. Johnson removes the gun from George and points it at Eva. She directs George to sit in the large chair in front of the desk. She instructs James to wrap George's hands with duct tape behind him and wrap his feet together. By the time this is done, Ms. Johnson can see the splotches on the grid getting closer to the point identified by Eva as the portal. She motions with the gun for Eva and James to walk to the door exiting the tech lab. She is confident no one will see them leave the house through the back door. There are no ATVs waiting at the end of the patio, so the three of them will have to walk across the back lawn and garden to the hedge. As they make their way across the patio at gunpoint, they walk right past the window of the spare bedroom where Zac is recuperating. Luckily, Zac is awake and happens to be distracted by shadows moving past his window.

He gets up from his bed and moves quickly to the window. He looks out to see Eva and James walking in front of Ms. Johnson. Ordinarily, he wouldn't have been too surprised to see them outside except one thing caught his attention immediately. Aunt Eva was walking. As he looks again, he notices that their body language isn't quite right. He decides to follow them without being seen. He puts on his pants and shoes and wraps a shirt around his shoulders buttoning the top button to keep it on. He quickly exits his bedroom and moves across the patio and down the lawn hiding behind anything he can find. When they get to the garden, Zac finds his choices of hidings places much improved.

When Eva, James and Ms. Johnson reach the hedge, Ms. Johnson immediately notices the rock. It appears to be so out of place that it occurs to her to be a marker. She motions for Eva and James to move towards the rock. It is obvious they will wait until Dawn exits the hedge through the portal. After several minutes have passed, Ms. Johnson looks up at the hedge when she hears a whistling sound. As she moves closer to the sound coming from the hedge, she can see the ripples ever so faintly. She backs up just in time for the ripples to part and watches Dawn and Bessie walk quickly from inside. Immediately, Dawn sees the gun in Ms. Johnson's hand.

"Nancy," Dawn says astonishingly, "What is this?"

Ms. Johnson points the gun at Dawn and motions for her to move away from the portal opening. She doesn't want Dawn to escape back into the hedge. Dawn moves away as Ms. Johnson circulates until her back is at the portal. At the very moment that Ms. Johnson is satisfied she has everything under control, Zac jumps out from a nearby rose bush.

"Purolarano," he says as he motions his good arm towards Ms. Johnson.

Ms. Johnson is hurled backwards into the open portal, gun and all. Surprised at the prospect of being saved by Zac's limited magicology, it occurs to Dawn that he may need assistance in closing the portal. Instinctively, she now completes the second part of the portal spell.

"Sinjoleckis," Dawn shouts and steps back to watch the portal close trapping Nancy Johnson inside the hedge.

THE END

Watch for Dawn's next adventure.